*ESPECIALLY FOR GIRLS*™ *presents*

# Split Sisters

## C. S. ADLER

Macmillan Publishing Company
New York

Collier Macmillan Publishers
London

To FRANK HODGE,
Upstate New York's Pied Piper of children's literature, with
thanks for all the good reading he has promoted.

Thanks to my young friends Stacy Sammo, who checked this
manuscript for gross adultisms and antique phraseology, and
Michael Roncevich, my computer expert. Also thanks to Sarah
Keating, my medical consultant.

This book is a presentation of **Especially for Girls**, Weekly Reader Books.
Weekly Reader Books offers book clubs for children from preschool through
high school. For further information write to:
**Weekly Reader Books,** 4343 Equity Drive, Columbus, Ohio 43228.

Published by arrangement with Macmillan Publishing Company.
Especially for Girls and Weekly Reader are trademarks of Field Publications.
Printed in the United States of America.

Macmillan Publishing Company, 866 Third Avenue, New York, N.Y. 10022
Collier Macmillan Canada, Inc.

Library of Congress Cataloging-in-Publication Data
Adler, C. S. (Carole S.)
Split Sisters.
Summary: When her parents decide to live apart, eleven-year-old Case tries to figure out a way
to keep the family together so she doesn't have to separate from her beloved sister.
[1. Sisters—Fiction] I. Title. PZ7.A26145Sp 1986 [Fic] 85-15411
ISBN 0-02-700380-9

# ·ONE·

I HAD TO GET to school early for volleyball-team practice; so I beat my sister to the bathroom. Then I went and did what I'd given her my solemn promise not to do again, and that made her so angry that she wouldn't speak to me all the while we were eating breakfast. I can't stand it when Jen won't talk to me. I got down on my knees and pleaded with her, but she wouldn't say one word. She just rinsed her dishes and left for high school. I felt awful. Jen's fourteen, three years older than me, and I worship the ground she walks on. I know that sounds corny, but it's true. Really. She's a nearly perfect person. I'm not so perfect. In fact, my mother calls me impossible, which I'm not. But I can see how after three years of Jen, Mother wouldn't take too well to an ordinary baby like me who yelled and broke things and was generally messy. She still braces herself when she sees me coming.

Well, after starting out bad, my day got worse. I ran upstairs to get my lucky cap with the fake false teeth on the brim and bumped into Mother on my way back downstairs.

"Forget something, Mom?" I asked her, because she looked fully equipped to leave for work in her pin-striped shirtwaist dress and medium heels, with shoulder bag and attaché case.

"Left a report on my night table," she said. She's always worked evenings on her budgets and statistical stuff, but lately she's also been taking reports to bed with her. You can guess how much time that leaves her for family life. My father—well,

1

really Gerry's my stepfather, but I call him Dad because that's how I feel about him—works for the same company. He's in Employee Relations and has to do all the training programs, but *he* leaves his work at the office at five o'clock.

Anyway, she noticed me.

"Are you planning to wear that outfit to school?" she asked me. She shouldn't frown. She looks about as square and wrinkle-browed as a bulldog when she frowns. Unfortunately, I look just like her.

"I've got volleyball practice this morning and a game after school."

"The shirt's indecent the way those arms are cut out, and the hat's ridiculous," she said.

She doesn't believe in tact. Jen's the tactful one in our family, but Mother just socks it to you, or anyway to me. I once asked Gerry if she's nice to people at work, and he thought I was being funny. "Of course she is," he'd said. "Your mother's a good-hearted person." He and I don't see Mother the same way.

Anyway, I was insulted. "This is my lucky hat," I said. "And I bought this T-shirt at a garage sale with my own money." It had yellow and purple stripes and cost me a quarter. If I needed a bra it would be indecent, maybe, but unfortunately I'm stuck with an underdeveloped eleven-year-old body.

"Change the shirt," Mother said.

"I'm going to be late," I said. "Mr. LaRow said he won't hold before-school practice if we can't get there on time."

"Get a blouse and take it with you," Mother said.

"Mother!"

"Arguing will make you later still." She stood there as calm as if she had all the time in the world, and even though I knew she was as anxious as I was to get going, I was the one who gave in. I yanked a blue checked shirt out of the closet and raced out of the house. Mother was getting into the car beside Dad.

"Can I have a lift to school?" I asked.

2

Mother hesitated, but Gerry said, "It's not far out of our way, Marian."

"All right," Mother agreed. "If you can manage not to be outrageous for the next ten minutes, Case."

I leaned over the back of the front seats and gave them a simultaneous hug. "Look at what nice parents you can be when you try," I said. It was the last time I was to feel good about them for a long time.

The problem of getting Jen to forgive me kept me busy during most of my morning class periods. My specialty is hearts, not just red ones with matching fat curves, but hearts with character. I draw them when I need to say important things to Jen, like that I'm sorry. I'd filled half my notebook with broken hearts and little hearts with weeping faces and bird-shaped hearts singing, "I'm so sorry," when my math teacher walked by my desk. I used to have a crush on him, but he doesn't look cute to me anymore since I found out how mean he is.

"Trash the hearts and try using your head for a change, Casey," he said to me. Now is that the way to talk to a good, if not great, student? And I haven't been talking out without raising my hand in class lately, either. I also got an evil eye from my sixth-grade homeroom teacher, but that could have been because she'd had another fight with her fiancé. We can gauge the progress of her love life by the looks she gives us.

By lunchtime I'd done a fair copy in full color of a top-hatted heart that I considered excellent. Norma, my best friend, had a dentist appointment. So I ended up sitting across the table from a girl who used to be my friend in third grade. She'd dropped me for a kid who owned a swimming pool. When she had tried to make up with me in fourth grade, I'd discussed with Jen what I should do.

"You could give her a second chance if you think she's changed," Jen had advised.

"She hasn't," I'd said, "but I could use an extra friend."

3

"Somebody you can't depend on?" Jen had asked.

I'd thought that one over. People should be loyal to each other. My sister and my friend Norma don't put on/off switches on relationships. Neither did I. "I don't really like her anymore," I'd told Jen.

"Then don't be her friend," Jen had said promptly. She's always been good at unmuddling me.

After school, I barely had time to show Norma the top-hat heart apology before she went to pick up her little brother from kindergarten. Usually we take turns walking each other halfway home—we live in opposite directions—but today Norma didn't have time.

"Mother needs help getting him to the doctor for his shots, Case," Norma apologized. "Listen, Jen's going to love your top-hat heart. Don't worry."

I walked home alone, feeling as if I'd spent the day in solitary confinement.

Jen was upstairs in our bedroom, and the closed door really scared me. All I could think was that she must still be angry at me for using her towel this morning. That was what I'd promised her I'd never forget not to do again, but it's hard to take this thing she has about private towels and toothbrushes seriously. I like to get as close to the people I love as I can. Do you know she even considered asking for her own room when we moved to Stamford four years ago? I talked her out of *that* fast.

"Who's going to be there if I wake up scared in the middle of the night?" I'd asked her.

"You're not a baby anymore, Case."

"But you're my security blanket," I'd told her. "And it's cozy to talk in the dark before we fall asleep, isn't it?"

She'd agreed, of course. I told you she was a perfect person.

I slid the pink and purple heart with the top-hatted cat weeping into a towel and saying, "I'm sooooo sorry," under the door. While I was waiting for Jen to notice it, I heard my parents'

4

voices coming up the stairs. That was strange. They both should have been at work. Unless somebody was sick. Was Jen sick? Was that why our door was closed?

I burst into the room yelling, "Jen, are you all right?"

She was sitting at her desk doing her homework, still dressed in school clothes. Jen doesn't have to climb into her sweat suit before snacking or risk plastering her clothes with banana chocolate flip like I do. Even though she's only a freshman in high school, she's got that polished grown-up look, and she's pretty, with delicate features. Mine look like a not-too-talented kid has been playing Mr. Potato Head with them.

"What's the matter with you?" Jen asked.

"Why'd you close the door?"

"So that I wouldn't hear Gerry yelling. They came home to have a private talk, they said, but whatever they're discussing is making him really mad."

She sounded scared, and I understood why. Our stepfather is an easygoing man. Mother's the one who gets excited and yells. I listened. I could hear Dad, all right. " . . . never think of anyone but yourself," he said, or shouted.

And then Mother answered something, and he said, "I am *not* envious. Do you think everyone has the same ambitions you have?"

"Please don't listen, Case," Jen said. "You'll just get yourself involved, and it's not your fight."

She was biting her lower lip, and she looked so upset that I said, "Don't worry. They're just communicating loudly." COMMUNICATION IS HEALTHY is a heading from a family-study unit we just did in social studies. "Are you still mad at me?"

"You mean about this morning? No," she said. "I was just annoyed because you'd promised."

"I know. I did, and from now on I'll never use your towel even if I can't find my own and I have to put dry clothes over a dripping-wet body and I can't get my hair dry and it's freezing

5

outside and I get pneumonia.''

"Good," Jen said without a smile. Mid-April's probably not the best time to arouse sympathy for possible chills and fever.

I stuck my head out our bedroom window, inhaling spring and admiring the forsythia bush, which looked like a burst of sunshine next to the detached garage. "You might as well read my note even if you're not mad at me," I said.

"One of your best," Jen judged after she looked over the card. "You gave that hat a lot of character."

"I thought it came out pretty well," I agreed. Art is one of my most favorite subjects. On the other hand, so is home ec., math, social studies, English and phys. ed. The only subject I hate is music, and we only have that twice a week for three months out of the year. We have art or home ec. the other months.

Jen added the drawing to the basket full of hearts I've given her, which she kept in the closet. I did my first heart in nursery school and presented it to Mother, but even at age three, I could tell Mother couldn't care less. My sister was the one who appreciated my artwork, so she got it all. Once when I was home sick, I counted up the hearts I've drawn for Jen, and, including little ones in borders, it came close to a thousand.

"How about a game of backgammon when you get your school-work done?" I asked next. Jen has a work-first, play-last policy, which is another way we're different.

"I'll try to get this book done for English fast," she promised.

"Okay, I'll go get a snack then," I said.

"Case, are you going to listen in?"

"Me?" I said as if it were the furthest thought from my mind.

They were in the kitchen. I tiptoed toward it with my ears primed and ready, and if that's eavesdropping—well, I got punished for it. First I heard Gerry say, "You're crazy. You know how I hate the city. No way will I let you move us there."

"Gerry, I've worked so hard for this promotion. Be reasonable."

6

"You be reasonable. You want to subject yourself to Mackey's bullying for the sake of a fancy title, go ahead. You can commute from here to New York City."

"That's what you call reasonable? Remember, when we moved to Stamford and bought this decrepit house, it was *your* idea of the good life, not mine. And I warned you then I'd only tolerate it so long as I didn't have to become a commuter. You've had four years here, and now it's my turn. My job's in the Big Apple and I want to be there, too."

"How anyone in his right mind could want to live in that city—"

"You don't have to go," Mother told him. "Stay here if you want."

"And what about the girls?" he said. "They love this place, too."

"Why should I have to take a couple of extra hours out of my day for travel time? I already have too few hours as it is, and with this new job—"

"With this new job you won't spend any time at all with me and the kids."

"Listen, Gerry," Mother said. "We're going to need the extra money if you really plan to quit your job."

"I'm not retiring, just changing careers."

"But you're not going to be making a living at this latest in your history of career changes," Mother said.

That's when Dad exploded and cursed. I covered my ears, and when I uncovered them he was saying, "Ever since I was a kid, I've dreamed of becoming a cartoonist. Don't you think it's time I tried?"

"Drawing cartoons is a kid's idea of a career, all right," Mother said, putting him down the way she does me. "How many people make a living at it?"

"Some do. How do you know I couldn't?"

"You can do what you want," she said, "but I'm moving to

New York."

"I thought we came home to discuss things," he said. "You're not discussing. You're handing out ultimatums. Well, forget it. If you want to move to the city, you can do it by yourself."

"Do you want a divorce?" Mother asked.

I couldn't stand any more. "Jennnnn!" I yelled and then burst into tears. My parents rushed out of the kitchen just as Jen came running down the stairs to my rescue.

"Case, you little sneak, you were listening in again," my mother accused. "Serves you right if we've upset you."

"Have a heart, Marian," Dad said. "Can't you see the kid's hysterical? Listen, Case, whatever you heard, remember that we love you."

"What's that got to do with anything?" Mother asked. "Case, what did you hear?"

"That you got a promotion," I wailed.

"You got the promotion, Mother? Congratulations," Jen said.

"*Finally,* somebody has a good word for me! Thank you, Jen," Mother said. "Yes, I've been offered the job of Manager of Financial Controls, working directly under Mr. Mackey. He's the controller in the head office. Isn't that wonderful?"

"I'm glad you got what you deserve after you've worked so hard for it," Jen said.

Mother was so moved, she got tears in her eyes. "Jen, darling," she said, "would you mind moving to the city?"

"New York City? Oh, I don't know," Jen said.

"I'd hate it," I put in, although nobody'd asked me.

"It wouldn't be like when we lived with Grandma in Brooklyn," Mother wheedled. "It would be interesting for you girls now. You'd be able to take in concerts and museum shows, and, Jen, you could go to a first-class high school."

"With a good computer program?"

"I guarantee it," Mother said.

Jen sighed and shrugged and said, "That's tempting." I could

8

tell she was resigning herself already.

"It's a trick, Jen," I screamed. "Don't say you'll go. Don't or something awful will happen to us."

Mother grimaced and suggested that Jen take me for a walk to calm me down. "Gerry and I need to do some more talking, and we'd better do it alone," she said.

"How long do you want us to stay away?" Jen asked.

"We'll have dinner at six. Okay? Thanks, honey."

"You're both crazy," I said, pulling away from my obliging sister, who was nudging me toward the front door. "Jen and I are part of this family, and we should be part of the decisions. Right, Daddy?" I took Gerry's hand in an appeal for justice, but I didn't get any, despite the sympathy in his round baby face that makes him look ten years younger than Mother instead of the three he actually is.

"Not now, Case," he said sadly. "You're just going to have to wait until your mother and I prepare the executive committee report."

He gave me a smile that made me want to stay and protect him, but Jen said, "Case, come on. We'll walk to the bay and sit on our rock."

Before I followed her out, I aimed a reproachful look at Mother, but she didn't even flinch.

"You weren't any help," I complained to Jen. I was walking backward so I could watch our grandmother house grow smaller. I'd nicknamed it the grandmother house the day we moved in when I was seven because it seemed old and dear the way grandparents in stories did. I still got comfort from it. "Why didn't you stick up for me?"

"Because you weren't going to help anything by getting involved," Jen said.

"Well, I'm not moving to New York City. No way. . . . And did you hear her, Jen? She said *divorce*. She said that word. We've got a good family going now, Jen. We can't just let them

9

wreck it.''

I turned around and walked beside her when the edge of the peaked roof disappeared and we had to cross the street.

''I don't know how they're going to work this one out,'' Jen said softly. ''They've always pulled in opposite directions. They fight and then make up with presents and breakfast in bed, but this time I wonder if either of them will give in.''

''I hope Gerry doesn't. I don't want to move to New York.''

''It's like they're getting farther and father apart, the way they're always sniping at each other,'' Jen said.

''What do you mean, sniping? Mother's the one who's mean.''

''Lately they both are,'' Jen said. ''Haven't you noticed? Gerry says it'd be nice if Mother would fit him into her schedule for an hour or two on a weekend, and Mother says how fortunate he is that his nature allows him to sit around doing nothing.''

''So.''

''So, that's like kids trading insults, Case.''

''You mean it's not just the promotion? Why didn't you warn me, Jen?''

''What for? Did you want to be unhappy sooner?''

''But I thought they loved each other,'' I said.

''Maybe they do. Maybe it will turn out all right.''

We turned onto the main road, where we had to walk single file because of all the cars illegally parked and no sidewalks. Our shortcut to the bay is after the second traffic light. From there we walk downhill through people's backyards.

''I hate it when I don't know what's going on,'' I grumbled. ''How can I fix anything if nobody tells me it's broken?''

''You can't fix this, Case. It's *their* marriage,'' Jen said.

''You're so sensible,'' I wailed. ''It's not going to save our family to be so sensible.'' When I get angry I even yell at Jen, but all she did was give me a sad-eyed look that made me feel worse.

10

# ·TWO·

THE HARBOR IN STAMFORD is our family's favorite destination for a walk. It's full of boats going to and from the Long Island Sound. Coast Guard, tug, fishing boat or fancy yacht—they're all fun to watch, although what Gerry and I like best is getting one of his boat-owning friends to take us out on the water. Mother enjoys speculating on how she could afford one of the expensive condos with a water view. Jen goes to the water to dream.

Of course, New York City has plenty of water, too, but the worst time in my life was when we lived in an apartment in Brooklyn before Gerry and Mother got married. Grandma was staying with us, baby-sitting us while Mother went to college for her M.B.A., which means Master of Business Administration. I don't remember my father. He died of leukemia when I was two. But I sure do remember living with Grandma. She is not a storybook character. She is a pill, the big nasty kind that makes you gag.

"I wonder what Grandma will say if and when they tell her what's going on," I said, after we settled down back-to-back on our rock. Jen was facing the breakwaters at the entrance to the harbor, while I faced the marina, where the action is.

"Grandma might be glad," Jen said. "Remember, she didn't want Mother to marry Gerry. She wanted her to concentrate on getting to be president of something."

"President of the U.S.A. would suit Grandma fine," I agreed. Grandma likes to have something to boast about. She'd wanted to push Jen into being somebody special, too. I was lucky. She'd decided long ago that I was a hopeless brat and hasn't wasted much energy pushing me. I remember Grandma trying to force Jen to learn how to sew. It had made me sick to see my sister get white and tremble as she fumbled with the simple skirt Grandma had insisted she make herself. Jen must have ripped and resewn that skirt every day for a month before Grandma gave up in disgust. It left Jen hating sewing so bad that, neat as she is, she'd go around stuck together with safety pins if I didn't do her mending for her. Sewing comes easy to me, the way computer-think does to her.

"Grandma means well," Jen said. My sister looks for positive things to say about people. I try, but not as hard as she does.

"I guess I won't count on Grandma," I said. "How else can we stop Mother from moving us to New York?"

"We can't stop her," Jen said. "She's been wanting to live in the city for years, and now that her new job is there, she'll move us."

"Don't talk that way," I said. "We're not family pets they can do what they want with. We've got rights. Besides, we've suffered enough for Mother's career by surviving five years with Grandma."

"You make Grandma out to be worse than she is," Jen said and reminded me of the most recent visit from her a couple of years ago. "She wasn't so bad then," Jen said.

"She was okay until she and Mother had that big fight over how to core the apple. Remember, that fight was Grandma's reason for flying back to Cincinnati steaming mad. Some reason," I said. "And when she lived with us, she was terrible. She picked on us all the time. You can't forget how she nagged you to speak up and smile and defend yourself. She made you stutter, didn't she?"

"But she didn't do it out of meanness, Case. She just thinks the world's a tough place and that kids should be trained for it."

"Even Mother complains that Grandma picks on her," I said. Jen gave up, letting me win the argument as usual.

I hoped Gerry was winning the one at home. Jen's mind must have been traveling in the same direction because she said, "I wish Mother wouldn't keep asking Gerry if he wants a divorce. Someday he might get angry enough at her to say yes."

"Gerry doesn't get angry," I said, before remembering that he *had* been angry today. "Besides, they like each other."

Jen shrugged.

"Well, don't they?"

"They haven't been having much fun together lately."

"That's because Mother's too busy with her job," I said. I watched a Sunday sailor trying to dock a Cheoy Lee that was more sailboat than he could handle. "Do you think she wants this promotion so she can be a big shot or for the money?" I asked Jen.

"I don't know," Jen said. "She already makes more than Gerry does. I guess she's more ambitious than he is. She told me once that she's never had a job that challenged her for more than the first few weeks. . . . Mother's got a lot of energy. I think the challenge is what appeals to her most, seeing how far she can get."

"Personally, I agree with Gerry," I said and quoted him: " 'Work's a necessity, but pleasure comes first because life should be enjoyed.' " A thought pushed me overboard. "Maybe they're not compatible." Divorce! Half the kids in my class have gotten divorced. Could I lose two fathers in one childhood? Unfair! "Jen, what if they got divorced?"

"Now, don't jump to conclusions," she said. "He hasn't taken her up on it yet."

"The least they could do is wait until we're grown up," I said.

"It'll be seven years until you're eighteen. That'd be a long wait, Case."

The Cheoy Lee ran over a dinghy and slammed into a dock.

Clothespin-sized figures went running toward it. "Whose side are you on, anyway?" I asked Jen.

"You know I'm always on yours," she said. "Unless you're being unreasonable."

"Being reasonable all the time is boring," I said. Also, you lose arguments by being reasonable enough to see the other fellow's point of view. That was one smart thing Grandma taught me.

"Do you think I'm boring, Case?"

"You? Never!" I was indignant that she'd even ask such a question. "You're excellent. In every way you're excellent."

Jen sighed. "I should have known better than to ask you. Even if I'm the most colorless person in the world, you think I'm wonderful because I'm your sister." Then she smiled and gave me a one-armed hug that tickled my insides happily.

"Do you think you're boring?" I asked.

"I must be," she said. "I'm the only girl my age who'd still rather be with her little sister than a boy."

I thought about it. The late afternoon sunlight was buttery, and the harbor water glistened so you didn't notice how dirty it really was. No, I couldn't fault Jen's wanting to be with me. I'd rather be with her than anybody else, too.

"Norma and I nearly gave Mr. Petowsky a heart attack in school today," I said, thinking it was time to cheer Jen up. She swiveled around to pay attention, already smiling. "We were bandaging each other up in first aid and Norma had to go to the girls' room. Well, we asked for permission, but the teacher didn't notice we still had our bandages on, and Mr. Petowsky sees us coming down the hall toward his office. 'What happened to you two?' he wants to know, like he's scared we're on our way to sue the school. We laughed so hard Norma nearly didn't make it to the bathroom in time."

"Did you let Norma copy your homework again?"

"No, she did her own today, but it's not really her fault, Jen.

She has to baby-sit her little brother, and he won't let her get anything done." A nasty comparison popped into my head and I asked, "Did you hate having to baby-sit me when I was little?"

"No."

"Really? You don't have to spare my feelings. Tell the truth. I know Grandma made you take me everywhere you went, and you got stuck at home with me instead of playing with kids your own age. I would have hated it if I'd been you."

A curl blew across Jen's smile. "I didn't mind," she said. "I didn't have friends outside of school, and you were always lovable."

"I wish Mother thought I was lovable," I said. "If she did, she wouldn't have named me Case. Sticking me with Grandma's maiden name proves Mother didn't even like me whan I was born. And last time I talked to her about changing it, she said Case suits me. She thinks I'm an object, not a person. Even dogs get people names like Sam and Sally." Jen wasn't listening. She'd heard the complaint too many times, I guess.

"I wonder if Mother will move us to New York City right away or wait until the term ends. It's only two months more," Jen said.

"Gerry *might* persuade her to stay."

"Not once she's made up her mind," Jen said.

"I'm not going. They can't make me move," I announced. "It took me forever to find a friend like Norma, and I'm not going to just up and leave her in the middle of the term. Good friends don't grow on trees, you know."

"I wouldn't mind switching schools if I could get into one with a good computer program," Jen said wistfully. "Some high schools in New York have time-sharing systems with access to a mainframe computer. You can have your own account and do really sophisticated stuff."

"Computers! I bet I have the only fourteen-year-old sister who's crazier about computers than boys." I stood up, feeling agitated because Jen was sliding right over to Mother's side without any resistance at all. "Let's go back," I said. "You've kept me out of their hair long enough." I was sorry I'd left Gerry to fight with Mother alone. He needed my support if he was going to stand up to her. "Come on." I said. "I want to see what they're up to."

"You probably won't like it," Jen said. She was right, of course.

. . .

"Come sit down in the living room, girls," Mother greeted us with ominous good humor. "And I'll tell you what we've decided."

"Where's Dad?" I asked.

"He offered to make dinner tonight–tuna-fish roulette, your favorite, Case."

Gerry calls it tuna-fish roulette because he puts in whatever ingredients he finds around. So far we haven't been killed, and it always tastes good. "How come Dad's making dinner instead of telling us with you?" I asked.

"Don't be so suspicious," she said. "What I'm going to say isn't so bad."

"I doubt that," I said.

"Case, cool it," Jen warned as Mother got the tight-lipped look that signaled the end of her patience with me.

"You are the worst smart-mouthed kid. I don't know how your teachers stand you," Mother said to me. "If you can't be civil, you can go up to your room and hear our decision from your sister later."

I pressed my lips together to keep from pointing out that it was Mother's decision, not "ours." Gerry didn't want to move. He liked our little old house and fooling around with his friends' boats, and he liked the company of his "girls," as he called Jen and Mother and me. The only thing he didn't like was doing Employee Relations, and who could blame him for that? It didn't

16

sound much better than Mother's job, which dealt with budgets and balances and business projections.

Jen and I sat side-by-side on the couch. I felt as if I were in the principal's office waiting to be sentenced to forty hours of detention. I clutched the pillow I'd quick-stitched for Mother's birthday in the sickening lavender and blue that she'd done up the upholstered furniture and curtains in and breathed deeply.

"First of all, there's nothing final about this," Mother said cheerfully. "It's just a trial separation."

"A trial separation? That's what you get before you get divorced." I groaned. The kid Norma and I liked last year had said, "My parents are separated," and the next thing was she left for Arizona with her mother because they got divorced.

"Relax, Case," Mother said, "and don't start jumping to conclusions and getting melodramatic. I said we're separating, and that's all it is. We're moving to New York because of my job, and Gerry's going to stay in Stamford and see how he likes being a cartoonist. If you don't like living in New York City, you can move back in with Gerry. Fair enough?"

"Does Grandma know?" I asked.

"Not yet. Why? Since when are you concerned about your grandmother? I thought you were as down on her as you are on me."

"Aren't you going to tell her?" I asked.

"Oh, I get it," Mother said. "You think Grandma will try and talk us out of it. Well, maybe she will, but she won't succeed. So you can forget that one."

"You can't do this to us," I said, struggling to keep from crying. Crying doesn't impress Mother. She usually turns me over to Jen as soon as I start to cry.

Mother looked calm. When she looks like that, I know it's useless to fight her. Better to wait and go for a sneak attack later. Suddenly I remembered a Monopoly game we'd played in this very room one stormy Saturday night. Mother had all the best property, and she had that smug look on her face while the rest of us scrambled to trade so we could build hotels and not go bankrupt. Then Gerry divided everything he had between Jen and me. He went to make us all popcorn, and Mother yelled that it wasn't fair, and Jen won the game.

"Let's all go to a movie now," Gerry had suggested.

"It's Saturday night, adult time," Mother had said. "Jen could baby-sit Case."

"But I like to have all my girls together," he'd said.

Mother had smiled a melting smile at him then. In her heart, she must like being a family, too, I thought—if she still had a heart, if it hadn't turned into a spread sheet or a financial report.

# ·THREE·

NOTHING MUCH HAPPENED FOR a while, or if it was happening, Gerry and Mother weren't talking about it where I could hear. I even began hoping that Mother had forgotten about her promotion and that we were going to be okay. Fat chance. We were finishing dinner one night when she announced, "This afternoon, I finally found an apartment that will do."

"What?" I jumped into high gear immediately. "You've been looking for apartments behind our backs? Well, good for you, but I'm not moving."

"Stay here with Gerry then, if you like, Case," Mother said stiffly.

"Well, I will if you make us move," I said.

"I'm *not* making you. Didn't you hear me? You can stay if the house means more to you than your mother does."

"Case," Jen warned, "you're hurting Mother's feelings."

"But what about Dad's? Why should she always get her own way?"

"To be fair, she hasn't yet," Gerry said quietly. "Living in Stamford was my idea. I hoped Marian could be weaned from the big city, but apparently she can't."

"So we're moving?" I asked him in confusion.

"I'm staying," he said quietly. "Will you stay with me, Case?"

"Sure," I said, adding my weight to his tug of war with Mother. "Jen and I'll stay. We like it here in Stamford."

"Jen's going with *me*," Mother said.

"That's decided already? Then you've been talking together

19

behind my back," I accused.

"We've considered the possibility that you might prefer staying with your father, yes," Mother said.

I saw the knife aimed at my gut. "You mean you're taking my sister away from me? You can't do that. You can't. No way are you going to divorce Jen and me." I stood up and threw the rest of my apple turnover at Mother and myself at Gerry, who was standing at the sink.

"Don't let her do it to me, Daddy. Save me. Please save me!" I guess you could say I was upset. When he put his arms around me and hugged me against his broad chest, I didn't even see that he was crying.

"My poor Casey, my poor little baby. I know just how you feel," he said. I noticed his tears then, but they didn't give me much hope. Like Jen, he's too quick to make the best of things. "Listen," he said, "you and I will have fun. We're going to move onto that cabin cruiser my friend Buddy owns, you know, the one at the marina that's been up for sale for a year? *The Jokester*."

"Appropriate name for a would-be cartoonist," Mother remarked.

"No," I said. "I changed my mind. I have to go with Jen."

"Listen," Gerry said, "you have to learn to do without Jen soon, anyway. In three years she'll leave for college. Just look at this as preliminary training."

"I'd rather be miserable in three years than now," I said.

"You're really making the best choice if you stay with Gerry," Mother said.

"Jen, say something!" I begged.

Her faced looked crumpled from hurting. "You know you'd hate the city worse than anything," she murmured.

"Why can't Mother go alone?"

"Because I need someone, too," Mother said.

"I'll kill myself," I said. "I'll run away from home."

"Look, Case," Mother reasoned, "if you stay with your father and Jen comes with me, we all gain something to balance what we lose. It really is the fairest way."

"I'm sorry, honey," Gerry said to me. "I really am."

And that was it. All he had to give me was sympathy. If Mother was going to be stopped, I had to do it myself. I went straight to bed. I do my best thinking in bed.

Jen came up after a while and collected her schoolbooks. "Case, I'm going to get my social studies homework done, and then we'll talk about it, okay?"

"Don't you care?" I raised my head from my pillow to ask.

"I hate it. You know I do. But it's only going to be temporary, Gerry says. Mother calls it a trial separation. Oh, Case, what can we do?" Then Jen started crying. I was horrified. I'm the one who does the crying in our family.

"We'll do something," I said. "I'll make Mother change her mind. You'll see. Don't cry, Jen. I'll fix it somehow." I even believed I would.

You know how some days look so sparkly that you're sure everything's going to go right? That's how it was the next morning. The birds were at an early-morning pep rally in the shade tree outside our open window, and Mother's electric toothbrush buzzed along with their chirps and chatter. I knew it was Mother in the bathroom because nobody else in our family needs electricity for brushing teeth. I inhaled a lungful of spring air and marched off to do battle.

Mother's almost as self-conscious about her bodily functions as Jen and doesn't enjoy bathroom conferences, but it's the only place I can be sure to catch her alone. She was flossing her teeth when I walked in. I said good morning and perched on the toilet seat.

"Couldn't you at least knock?" she said.

"You should have locked the door if you didn't want company," I told her. "I need to talk to you. Okay?"

"I'm listening."

"Don't you care what happens to Jen and me?" I asked.

"Of course I care."

"But you're letting us be separated."

"You and Jen can still see each other on weekends," she said.

"How?"

"By taking a train into the city and then a subway up to our apartment. Or vice versa—she can come to you."

"It'd take hours."

"I thought you'd do anything to be with her. What's an hour or two?"

"Each way, and what about during the week when I need to talk to her?"

"Telephone."

"Maybe I'll change my mind about liking New York," I said, knowing Mother wasn't going to change hers.

"Actually, it'll work out well this way, Case," Mother said. "You wouldn't have to leave Stamford or Norma or your school. You can get a school bus near the marina and keep house for Gerry, and you and he can cook up all those revolting dishes you both like."

"Why can't we stay here in the house?"

"Because we can't afford both the house and an apartment in the city while Gerry's not bringing in an income. If we're lucky, maybe we can rent the house, although personally I'd be glad to get rid of it."

"You'd sell this house?"

"Why do you always make me feel like the wicked witch, Case? Why is your sympathy always with Gerry and never with me?"

I wasn't going to get sidetracked by answering her. Instead, I asked, "Could you just tell me how come you want Jen, but not me?"

22

"Oh, come on, Case. You know I want you both, but you don't really want to come, and it happens that the best apartment I could afford has only one bedroom. And while I can get Jen in a better public high school than she's got here, you'd have to go to a neighborhood school on such a bad street that I'd be scared you'd get mugged or worse. You're better off here."

"You could send me to private school, couldn't you?"

"No, I could not. My pay increase wasn't that terrific. Now don't try to make me feel guilty. The fact is, you're happy here, and the separation is just temporary. Think how Gerry would feel if we all left him! He needs you, Case. You made the right decision."

She'd given me so many reasons it made me suspicious. "You don't want me," I said. "Why can't you just be honest and admit you hate me?"

"Because I don't. It's true you're an awful kid," she said with a grin, "but I have faith you'll grow out of it someday. Snakes shed their skins, so you might possibly—"

"If I get down on my knees and beg you, will you let me come?" I interrupted her to ask and promptly dropped to my knees on the blue tiled floor. "Please, Mother!" I clasped my hands to show that I was at her mercy.

"Yuck," Mother said. "Just yuck to that kind of blackmail." She grabbed her robe from the hook on the back of the door, draped it around her and marched to the parental bedroom, which is off limits to us when the door is shut, under penalty of no television for a month. Mother shut the door hard.

Obviously the spring air hadn't affected her at all. I padded downstairs to see if I could do anything with Gerry, instead. He was in the kitchen, staring out the window instead of at the newspaper propped against his coffee cup. All you see from our kitchen window is the detached garage with its door stuck open and the rusty old swing set he put up for Jen and me. So I figured he was thinking, not looking.

"It's awful, Daddy, isn't it?"

For answer he held out his arms, and I curled up on his lap and tucked my head under his chin the way I used to. Right away I felt better. We stared out at the garage together, and I began my pitch. "We're a happy family, aren't we, Dad?"

"Were," he said.

"Well, Mother's the only one not happy. So why can't she just move away and leave the rest of us here together?"

"That's not how she wants it, and it wouldn't work out economically. Now that I'm not bringing in any money, the only way we can afford two households is for me to live on Bud's boat. I can live on it rent-free in exchange for getting it in shape to sell, he says. Won't it be fun, just you and me?"

He looked so sad and pleading that I wanted to agree, but I couldn't risk sympathy. "Not if I can't have Jen with me," I said.

He took a deep breath and told me, "Case, even if I were willing, your mother wouldn't let me keep both Jen and you. I know you're nuts about your sister, but I sort of hoped that you loved me, too."

"You're my most favorite parent," I assured him, "but Jen's my most necessary person in the world. You listen okay, but half the time you don't understand what I'm upset about. Remember when I got kicked out of gym for not having socks? You thought it was funny, but Jen went and explained to the teacher about the dryer burning up. Please, Daddy, talk Mother into letting Jen and me stay together."

He sighed and shifted me off his knees. Sure, I'm on the plump side, but he's no lightweight, and he didn't have to push me off like that. He started mumbling about the boat and how it was basically a beauty and how now we'd spend a lot of time together because being a cartoonist wouldn't take up his whole day.

Then he tried to win me over from another angle. "It's my last chance at a career that suits me, Case. The business world

24

is not for me. Before I met your mother, I'd already dropped out of law school and given up on teaching. Maybe I'll wind up a failure at everything, but this cartoon thing is something I've wanted to try all my life. Only, I need someone to stick by me. If I have to hack it alone, I'll get too depressed to be creative.''

I had to bite my lip to keep from saying, sure I'd stick by him. I love Gerry a lot, but I love my sister more. "Jen and I could share the bow bunks," I said. "We wouldn't eat much. I bet you could talk Mother into letting you keep both of us. We'd do all the housekeeping, and you'd have us both for company. Doesn't that sound good?''

"For you and me, sure. But you're forgetting your sister gets seasick. How's she going to sleep on a boat that rocks in its slip when the wind kicks up?''

"She can take pills for motion sickness.''

"Case, you know I couldn't talk your mother into letting me keep both of you.''

"I'll do it then," I said.

"Just remember that I need you very much, honey.''

I didn't want to hear that from him. He's an adult. He can find somebody else. But a kid like me has no choice. I have to do what the adults in charge decide. Until you're grown up, you're helpless. It was a scary thought and it made me mad. I wished I could hire a lawyer to keep Mother and Gerry from separating me from Jen. I wished I could charge them both with unfair treatment of a minor. Well, I'd tried talking to them. Next came action.

I ran upstairs to get dressed for school. Jen had a late-morning class and was still asleep. She looked so sweet and innocent with a halo of hair on her pillow and long eyelashes curling on her cheek. I wanted to wake her and tell her that Gerry had said he needed me. At least *he* doesn't go around telling me what a rotten kid I am. Even if Mother is joking, it hurts my feelings, and how do I know she doesn't mean it? She certainly does get along better

25

with Jen. Well, Jen's practically an adult. And Mother's quick to admit she isn't good with kids. She does what a mother is supposed to do, like getting our teeth checked and feeding and clothing us, but she prefers adult company to ours. Her job and going to concerts with Gerry and eating out—that's what she enjoys most.

I let Jen sleep and hurried into the wrap skirt Mother had bought me in three different colors because it makes me look thin. Norma would have some good ideas about how to keep Mother from splitting the family, but we'd only have ten minutes before class to talk even if both Norma and I made it to homeroom early today.

I've been in and out of a few friendships since kindergarten. Most didn't work out, starting with a girl who borrowed my crayons in kindergarten. I had to beat her up to get them back, and she told on me to the teacher. In second grade I met a girl named Lois who was only my friend when nobody she liked better was around. That same year, Mother married Gerry, and Grandma moved back to Cincinnati, where she was born. The rest of us moved to Stamford, where I made friends with a nice boy, but he changed schools at the end of the year.

Norma is the first kid I've ever stayed friends with. She's never given away my secrets, or chosen somebody else to work with in class. She even stood back-to-back in the school yard with me in fourth grade when I was the only girl the boys hadn't sprayed with red paint. She helped me beat up three of them even though *her* skirt had already gotten sprayed. Norma stands by me when I get in trouble with teachers, too. I get in trouble mostly because I'm the one who speaks up and tells them what they're doing wrong. She says the only thing she doesn't like about me is the way I talk to my mother.

"You're supposed to respect your parents," Norma's always telling me. "My mother would smack me if I talked back the way you do."

Once I told Norma that Gerry is the best thing my mother ever

26

did for me besides producing Jen.

"Your stepfather's a nice man," Norma agreed. "But your mother's your mother."

On the way to school I wondered if Norma would still think Mother deserved my respect now. Norma's strong on family. She has four brothers, one younger and three a lot older than herself. That's why she never fusses if we can't get together. She can always find someone at home to do things with. All I have is Jen.

"My family's splitting in half," I announced as soon as Norma and I were seated on the air-vent covers next to the back windows. It was the best spot to avoid the kids who were busy shooting paper covers from straws they'd taken from the lunchroom. Briefly I told Norma about my mother's plan.

"All that just because she got promoted?" Norma asked. "Are you sure they're not doing it because they don't love each other anymore?" Her mother doesn't work; so it's hard for Norma to understand how my mother is.

"What's Jen say?" Norma asked next.

"She just feels bad quietly," I said. "So what should I do?"

"I suppose you already argued with them?"

"You know I did," I assured her. "Now I have to *do* something. But what? Killing myself is too gross, and I'd be scared to run away from home."

Norma considered. Where I get too excited and emotional to think straight, Norma keeps a steady course. She squinched her face up. When she thinks, her lips disappear. Her face is long and thin, and my mother says she's homely, but I like her looks. She looks like Norma.

"You could get sick, very, very sick," Norma suggested. "Then they might feel guilty about what they were doing to you and stop."

"What should I get?" I asked, liking the idea immediately. "It has to be worse than a stomach ache but not so bad I can't

27

get well. Your brother isn't still contagious, is he?''

"Chicken pox wouldn't do it," Norma said. "And the weather's too nice for pneumonia. How about poisoning yourself?''

"No, thanks. . . . With what?''

"I don't know," Norma said, but I knew she'd think of something.

Ms. Hawkins, our homeroom teacher, walked into the room smiling. Her glazed look meant she and her fiancé were loving each other again. I wished my mother'd look a little glazed once in a while. The class began drifting toward their seats as Ms. Hawkins picked up her attendance cards. Norma took her seat in the back of the room promptly. I was slower to claim mine in the front row. I'd been moved there for talking to Norma too much. Nothing to look at up front but the chalkboard. Nothing on that but ''don't forget'' notices and somebody's leftover hangman game.

How could I get sick seriously, but not too seriously? The school library must have a book on poisons. What I needed was a dose big enough to make Mother believe I meant it when I said I couldn't be separated from Jen. My only other idea was to burn the boat Gerry and I were supposed to live on. It had been sitting in the marina since last summer with a ''For Sale'' sign on it, and nobody wanted it, but even so, I couldn't do that to Dad's friend Buddy, who was a nice guy if a little flaky. Maybe I could burn our house down instead. That'd serve Mother right. But burning boats and houses was too crazy. Other people could get hurt. Besides, it would be a rotten thing to do to Gerry. Also, I couldn't burn down the only house I'd ever been happy in. Four years of being a happy family—that wasn't even half my life. And now Mother was scuttling the whole thing because of a promotion to the head office. I couldn't help it: Instead of being promoted, I wished she'd been left back.

The bell rang, and we shuffled across the hall to math class, where I had to concentrate too hard to do any more thinking.

28

# ·FOUR·

MOTHER DISAPPEARED INTO HER new job, and I mean disappeared. What with working late and commuting the extra hour forth and back every day, all I got was glimpses of her now and then. She was putting pressure on Gerry to sell the house instead of renting it, but he was doing a pretty good job of stalling her, I thought. Meanwhile, I was investigating poisons. It didn't take me long to decide they weren't safe even in small doses, but neither Norma nor I came up with a better idea.

Mother's birthday was Sunday. Saturday morning I was sitting at the kitchen table painting flower hearts of lavender and blue on a card that was to go with the half slip Jen and I had bought Mother. Jen was sitting across from me, waiting to write the inside greeting. She had to because I refused to write anything nice to the person who was planning to ruin my life. I jumped and spilled the paint when Mother stuck her head in the kitchen and said, "You girls have less than an hour to get your room picked up. A real-estate woman is coming to look us over."

"You're going to rent the house out from under us?" I asked.

"Worse," she said grimly. "We're selling it, Case. We need the money."

"And Gerry agreed?" I should have known better than to let him fight Mother by himself.

"May's the best time to sell houses," Mother said, as if that explained anything. "Besides, Case, the faster we do it, the less it'll hurt."

29

"Hurt who less? Can't you give me time to adjust before you make me homeless?" I reached for the paper towels to mop up the paint, and the bowl of cereal Gerry had set on the counter sailed to the floor and shattered.

"I'll certainly be glad when she grows out of this stage," Mother said to Gerry, who was poking though a drawer for his cereal spoon.

"I think that was an accident, not a dramatic gesture," Gerry said in my defense.

"Dad!" I cried. "How can you just let her sell this house?"

He shut the drawer, and I saw little pinch lines at the end of his lips. "What's the matter with you, Case?" he said. "Would you want me to stand in your mother's way? Why, with her efficiency and lack of concern for people's feelings, she's sure to make the top rung of the executive ladder, and won't we be proud of her then!"

I'd never heard him so sarcastic. He'd always talked as if Mother was a terrific lady, interesting and dynamic. He'd even admired how successful she was at work when she got raises and he didn't. And, judging by the compliments he gave her, he thought she looked good, too. I turned to Jen, but she was busy mopping up the milk and shredded wheat I'd dropped on the floor. "I'm not going to help sell this house," I said. "I'm going back to bed, and if a real-estate lady wants to see my room, she can see it messy." I turned my back on them and left.

Nobody was going to help me. Jen would clean up after me, but she wouldn't fight by my side, and Gerry's sarcasm wouldn't stop Mother. I'd have to do it all myself. But do what? Getting sick, the way Norma and I had planned, wasn't likely to halt the house sale.

For once my brain worked fast. Before the doorbell rang and I heard the real-estate lady's voice, I knew what to do. I got dressed and even made my bed and picked up the clothes that were lying around. They were all mine, of course. Jen's neat. I could see her in the backyard. She was sitting in the lounge chair under the tree holding a book, but she wasn't reading. She was staring into the forsythia bush. If Jen's upset, she just stares. When I got downstairs, Gerry was nowhere in sight. Mother was sprinkling charm over a chunky, red-headed woman who was full of freckles and enthusiasm. I perked up my lips for a sweet, shy look. Anyone who knew me would know it was fake, but the saleslady didn't know me.

She spotted me in the doorway and said, "Well hi, there. You a member of the family or just visiting?"

Mother introduced us and said, "Case isn't feeling too well today. Weren't you going to stay in bed, dear?"

"I'm okay now," I said, and sidled to the couch. I sat down and leaned my head on Mother's shoulder. She was suspicious, but had no choice but to let me cuddle up and stay.

"Case, if Mrs. Delaney needs to show the house when I'm not home, you let her in, okay? Or if she calls, you let in any other salesperson she might send."

I nodded agreeably.

"Rough on a kid to have to move. I bet you hate it, don't you, honey?" Mrs. Delaney said.

I shrugged and smiled as if I didn't mind too much.

"Well, I guess that about wraps up the arrangements," Mrs. Delaney said to Mother. "Now if I can just have a look-see at the house and yard, I'll go and get things rolling for you at the office." She turned to me. "Would you like to give me a guided tour, honey? Your mother's got a meeting she had to make."

"I don't mind," I said, and looked at Mother, who was studying me, trying to figure out what I was up to. I held my breath, hoping that she wouldn't be able to read my mind the way she sometimes could. I was in luck. She looked at her watch and nodded reluctantly.

"Don't let her talk your ear off," she said to Mrs. Delaney.

"She's a talker?" Mrs. Delaney sounded surprised.

"Behave yourself, Case," Mother said to me with an "or else" in her voice. Then she got her purse and took off.

I asked where Mrs. Delaney would like to look first.

"Well, I've pretty much seen the downstairs, unless you know some secret compartments your mother's not aware of."

"No," I said, all dumb innocence. "Nothing special downstairs, unless you want to see the basement. It's not flooded now."

"Is it usually flooded?"

"Only when it rains hard. But nothing's down there anyway except the furnace and the washing machine and dryer."

Mrs. Delaney made a note on the pad she was carrying. "Anything else go wrong when it rains?" she asked.

"No, except the roof leaks, but that's just in the attic and you can put pots up there and catch it before it goes through the ceilings."

"Case, are you putting me on?" Mrs. Delaney asked.

I looked at her wide-eyed. "I love this house," I said sincerely. "It's the nicest house I ever lived in."

"Oh, okay." Mrs. Delaney smiled at me reassuringly. "And you have nice neighbors?"

I led the way up the stairs to the parents' oversized bedroom. It took up one side of the house while the stairwell, bathroom, storeroom and Jen's and my bedroom took the other. "The neighbors don't bother *me,*" I said, "even if they are a little crazy."

"How are they crazy?" Mrs. Delaney asked with a frown.

"Oh, it's no big deal, really. They howl. Or at least my parents say that's what makes the eerie noises we hear at night. I thought it was ghosts, but my family doesn't believe in ghosts."

"Any problems with the bathroom?" Mrs. Delaney asked, looking in and peering at the cracked tiles above the tub, which Gerry had said he was going to replace when he got around to it.

"I don't know what the plumber said, but Mother turned kind of green after he talked to her."

"Hmmm." Mrs. Delaney wasn't smiling anymore. She glanced out our bedroom window at the backyard, where Jen was reading in the lounge chair. "There's not enough yard for *it* to have any problems," Mrs. Delaney muttered.

"It's small, but it's nice unless the wind's blowing the wrong way and you smell the sewage leak. My parents don't think it's ours—the leak that makes the smell, I mean."

"Well, thanks, honey, you've been a big help," Mrs. Delaney said at the front door where we were saying good-bye. "Your mother was right; you're a talker." She smiled and headed for her car with the notebook tucked under her arm.

I felt bad. Even though I'd been sneaky in a good cause, being sneaky is not my usual thing. So I headed for the backyard to squeeze some comfort from my sister.

I leaned on the back of Jen's chair and asked her what she was reading.

"A French novel," she said. "I have to record my favorite chapter on tape for Mr. Duchamps. I'll die if he plays it in class."

"Don't worry," I said. "He probably won't have time, and even if he does, you'll sound fine. Didn't he say you have a good accent?"

"I'm sure to mispronounce *some* words, Case."

"You'll sound better than anybody else, anyway." I assured her. She'd had a crush on Mr. Duchamps all year. I got crushes on teachers, too, but not weird-looking ones with big noses and bad posture like Mr. Duchamps. "Jen, I think I may have gone too far," I said.

"At what?"

"At saving our family from splitting in half."

"You couldn't go too far if you could save us from that. What'd you do?"

"Well. . . ." I hesitated. No telling when Jen's principles would get in the way of her sympathy. "Well, I exaggerated some of the not-so-good things about the house to the real-estate lady."

"Do you think she believed you?"

"I don't think she'd consider selling our house to a friend of hers now."

"If your conscience is bothering you, you'd better confess to Mother. Or Dad, at least. He'd be easier on you."

"Right, I'll confess to Dad. Where did he go?"

"Down to the marina to check out Buddy's boat. I don't think he wanted to be around when the real-estate woman came."

I decided not to follow him down to the marina. No point in rushing into a confession when I wasn't sorry for my sin.

"I was thinking," Jen said. "If worst came to worst, Grandma might take us both in."

I couldn't believe what I'd just heard. "Move to Cincinnati and live with *Grandma*? You'd do that for me?"

"I don't know if I could really do it," Jen said. "It's just one possibility. . . . I don't want to lose you, either, you know."

"Why?" I asked. I knew I needed Jen. I never thought she might need me as much.

"Because," she said, and looked embarrassed, "you're the one who makes me smile. You make me happy, Case."

I caught my breath and told her, "That's the nicest thing you've ever said to me." Then I dashed for the house so that she wouldn't see me bawling like a baby.

Gerry was in the kitchen eating leftovers from a plastic container when I found him late that afternoon. "Dad, you don't want to get separated, right?" I began. My guilt had had plenty of time to cool.

"Right," he said. "But I'm not going to let your mother run roughshod over me, either. The way I want to live counts, too, Case."

"But you wouldn't object to something that would slow Mother down, would you?"

He looked at me carefully before he said, "I'd object to vi-

34

olence, illegality, criminality and general unethical behavior—in principle, that is. What did you do?"

"I stretched the truth a little, that's all."

"Would you care to explain further?"

"Well, let's put it this way," I said. "I don't think Mrs. Delaney's going to be all that eager to sell our house."

"You got to the real-estate person your mother brought in?" He sounded surprised.

"I think so."

He grinned. Then he finished the cold leftover noodles and shredded beef, aimed his fork at me and said, "Something must be wrong with my hearing today. I didn't hear a word you said just now. You wouldn't care to repeat it, would you?"

"Not unless you want me to."

"I don't want you to," he said. "Shall I whip up some banana flips for us?"

We made one for Jen, and I served it to her in the backyard. She was murmuring French into a microphone connected to the tape recorder she'd borrowed from school. "He's on our side," I told her when she put her hand over the microphone long enough to thank me for the flip.

"You're not going to tell Mother?" she asked.

"Why should I?" I said. "Mother shouldn't have everything her way."

"She doesn't, Case. You blame everything on her, but the truth is she would have moved us all to New York, but Gerry wouldn't go. It's his fault, too."

"Why should he live in the city if he hates it? If she wants that job so bad, why doesn't she just commute?"

"I have a feeling they're mad at each other about more than that," Jen said.

"What, then?"

"I don't know exactly, but they still seem to love each other a little."

"Yeah, I'll bet," I said. Again I wondered what Grandma was going to say when Mother finally broke down and told her.

. . .

We found out that evening. Grandma made her weekly phone call at six, right in the middle of dinner. She always does that, even though Mother keeps asking her not to call between five-thirty and seven. Tonight all Grandma was interrupting was chef's salad and French bread. Mother beat me to the phone.

"Yes, we are eating dinner," Mother said. "What do you mean, irregular lives? That's ridiculous. . . . Weekends are different, of course, if we're going out somewhere, but what's that got to do . . . Mother, did you call to fight with me or to find out how we are? . . . Fine, everybody's fine. And how was your week? . . . You always say terrible. Yes, I know being a companion to a senile old lady isn't the easiest job in the world, but you're good at it, and you always say how glad you are to have the job. . . . Yes, of course, I think it's good you find work even though you didn't have the benefit of a college education. . . ."

So far the conversation was familiar. Grandma had a thing about the importance of education. It was like she was jealous of Mother for being well educated, even though it was Grandma who'd always told her she should be. One of Grandma's big lines was, "I didn't have your benefits, after all." She'd also once cross-stitched a sampler that said, "Pride goeth before a fall," and given it to Mother for her birthday.

"Do you want to talk to your grandchildren?" Mother said. "Sure, they're both here. *Of course* they want to talk to you, Mother."

I went first. "Hi, Grandma. How are you?" I said as Mother retreated to the table with a sigh of relief.

"As all right as I can be living here all alone in this city with no family nearby. When are you going to make time in your life to come visit your old grandma?"

"I don't know," I said. "Everything's confused right now

36

because Mother is separating us.''

Grandma's ''What!'' was so loud that Mother threw up her hands and sank in her seat. I knew she wouldn't be down for long, though. As soon as the phone call was over, she'd make me pay for telling on her.

''Let me speak to your mother again,'' Grandma said, and I handed over the receiver, avoiding my mother's glare.

''I was *going* to tell you,'' she said to Grandma. ''Of course, I was, but I didn't want to worry you before everything was arranged. . . . No, not divorced, just a separation. It was a mutual decision. I got a promotion. . . . Well, I'm going to work for the controller in the head office, and Gerry absolutely refuses to consider living in the city, and I can't stand being a suburbanite anymore. . . . No, there's nothing I'm not telling you. . . . Yes, of course, I've considered the effect on the girls. They'll be fine, Mother. They're tough cookies, like you and me. . . . No, I don't mean to say you're a. . . . No, Mother. Listen, if you're going to start yelling, I'm hanging up. I refuse to listen to you if you're going to sound like that. I'm a grown woman, and I don't have to take that kind of . . . . No!'' And the receiver went bang.

''You really did it. You really got me good, you rotten kid,'' Mother said to me. Her face was so red that I began backing out of the kitchen.

''Jen, can you do the dishes for me tonight?'' I called before I ran. It wasn't that I couldn't take my punishment, but I really needed time to think about what I'd just done. Normally, Grandma is the enemy. I didn't know whether she'd be a good ally or make things worse for Jen and me.

For safety's sake, I retreated all the way to our rock near the harbor.

It was the kind of evening Jen loves, with a dim milky sky and lavender clouds on the horizon. Some of the boats coming past the breakwater already had their running lights on, and the lighthouse's flashing beam was skimming the water. I like mornings, when everything's new, better than ends of days. Grandma would probably prefer high noon. It's the best time for shootouts, and Grandma would have made a great Annie Oakley. Not that she's ever shot anybody with a gun, but she's a deadeye with words. Amazing that Jen would even consider going to live with her.

When Gerry talked Mother into marrying him, I was seven years old, and he'd been part of my life since before kindergarten, when he and Mother got to be friends. To me Gerry was the hero who'd rescued Jen and me from Grandma. The little house Mother and he bought in Stamford may have looked shabby squeezed between bigger houses on the old street, but it seemed wonderful after the apartment in Brooklyn we'd shared with Grandma. Our house didn't have any of the problems I'd told Mrs. Delaney it had. Oh, it'd had a few small accidents. The washing machine had flooded the basement when the hose burst, and there had been a smell in the backyard from somewhere last year, and the roof did leak once, but Gerry patched it. It's really a happy-ever-after house—or it had been.

Sitting on the rock and staring at the harbor, I tried to think about what I should do next to block Mother's plan, but my brain fidgeted instead of producing.

Tomorrow, after Mother's birthday brunch at the pancake house, I was going on a bike hike with Norma and her family. Jen was invited if she wanted to go. Probably she wouldn't. She'd rather lie around reading. One reason our family doesn't do much together is that eating out is the only thing we all four enjoy. What Jen likes best is fooling around with computers. It's funny that we're so close and yet so different. Our school has some Apples, and about all I've done is learn to play a couple of games on them. What *I* really and truly like best is home ec. Yeah, I know, cooking and sewing—not that I want to be a housewife. Maybe I could become a chef or a dressmaker. Although I like boats, too. I'm good at boats because I'm good with my hands.

38

Too bad Jen gets seasick so easily. It would be fun to spend the summer with Gerry on *The Jokester* if Jen were with us. I wouldn't miss Mother much. Although she's all right in her way. She's excellent in an emergency. And she knows how to fix people kinds of things, like when my third-grade teacher wanted me out of her class because she couldn't make me stop talking and like when I got into a fight trying to keep kids from picking on a wimpy new kid. Mother is what you'd call dependable—not easy to get along with, but very solid. We're such a good family, all of us together. That's the thing. That's what I have to make Mother understand. If only I could think of a way to do it.

# ·FIVE·

MOTHER DIDN'T GIVE ME such a hard time for my news flash to Grandma. Jen said that was because Grandma had called back while I was at the rock and wopped Mother hard with her broomstick. All Mother said to me when I returned was, "I thought you were mature enough to keep a secret, Case."

"You didn't say it was a secret," I said. "Are you ashamed that you're ruining our family?"

"Oh, kid, you really know how to dish it out. I don't know who you learned that from, unless it was me," Mother said. She walked away, looking weary. I snuggled between Jen and Gerry to watch a movie on cable. It was a gross and gory spy story, nothing I'd watch by myself.

In the morning we did the birthday brunch at the pancake house, being so polite to each other that we might as well have been strangers. The Belgian waffles were delicious, but they didn't change Mother's mind any better than Grandma had. Mother's as stubborn as I am. Jen says Mother and I are alike in a lot of ways. If we are, you'd think we'd get along better than we do, wouldn't you?

It was one of those puff-ball-cloud afternoons when everybody's tulips seem to be in bloom and there's enough breeze to make bike riding a pleasure. The weather made me cheerful as I rode my old three-speed to Norma's. Her next oldest brother, the silent one, was setting a bike in the rack on top of the family van as I cruised up. I said, "Hi," and handed over my bike to fit in

40

the remaining space. Norma's mother helped him lift it. She'd been a ski instructor and was still athletic-looking, despite having so many kids and being middle-aged. "Isn't it a great day for a bike ride?" she asked.

Norma came out of their big old colonial, which is even more run-down than our house. She was towing her little brother, who was crying and wouldn't say hello to me.

"What's the matter with Pooh Bear?" I asked Norma as we climbed in the back of the van together.

"He got invited to a party, but Mother made him come with us. The party was only going to last an hour, and the lady wouldn't keep him longer."

"Poor Pooh. Is he going to sulk all afternoon?"

"He might. Pooh Bear's a champion sulker." Norma said that with pride.

In the half-hour ride to the park, I filled Norma in on how I'd sabotaged the house sale and enlisted Grandma to our side. "And the best thing was that Jen said she'd be willing to go live with Grandma if that was the only way she and I could stay together," I boasted.

"But doesn't your grandma live way out in Ohio?" Norma asked. "You can't move to Ohio. You're my only friend, Case," Norma said. She isn't given to mush. So I didn't embarrass her by reacting, but I was really pleased that she'd said that.

"We've got to figure out another way," I said.

"I've been thinking," Norma said. "How about a mental illness? That'd be easier than faking anything physical."

"Mental illness. You mean I should go crazy?"

"No, just act crazy. Who's to tell if you are or not?"

"They'd send me to a psychologist," I pointed out.

"If you did it in school, they'd send you to the school psychologist. I don't think he knows much."

"He doesn't?"

"Remember when I got my period the first time and I was so

41

mad?'' Norma said. ''Ms. Hawkins couldn't figure out why I wouldn't talk to anybody. So she sent me to Mr. Belloti, and I was embarrassed and told him I was upset because I'd had a fight with my brother. So he believed me and lectured me for an hour on brothers and sisters getting along. You start acting funny in homeroom, and I bet you Ms. Hawkins ships you right off to Belloti.''

''But everyone will know.''

''So what's more important, what kids think about you or staying with your sister?''

I didn't have to answer. Norma knows how I feel about Jen. We got to the park and set off single file down the narrow asphalt path through the woods. Norma's brother was first, next her mother and Pooh Bear—still looking mad—then Norma and, last, me. I was busy thinking.

After we rumbled over a wooden bridge high over a stream, I sped up to ride beside Norma. ''How would you do it?'' I asked.

''Where we lived in South Carolina, a lady used to run out of her house without any clothes on, and it turned out she was crazy.''

''I'm *not* running around naked in homeroom,'' I said.

''How about screaming, then? You could just begin screaming, 'I can't stand it. I can't stand it,' and keep it up until they take you away,'' Norma said. ''I saw that on TV.''

''Can't you be crazy without stripping or screaming?'' I asked. I imagined myself hiding under my desk and pretending I thought bombs were going to fall on the school. Then I saw myself just slumping to the floor and moaning pitifully, ''I can't go on living without Jen.'' That might do it. Mr. Belloti would call up Mother and tell her I was upset about the separation. Of course, that wouldn't be news to Mother, but having a school psychologist tell her might impress her.

''You know a way to really get to your mother?'' Norma asked. ''If you attempted suicide. Even if she does care more about her

42

job than you, she wouldn't want your death on her conscience, would she?"

"You're right, Norma," I said and nearly swerved into her bike as I considered it. Suicide would be even more effective than getting sick. "That'd do it. . . . But how am I going to commit suicide in homeroom? Shoot myself in the head with a paper clip? I don't want to get hurt, after all."

"No, of course not. You know what we could do? I could tell Ms. Hawkins that you're acting strange. Then she'd send you to Belloti, and the kids probably wouldn't even know. You could tell him you're thinking of killing yourself. Just thinking about it should be enough."

"It wouldn't be enough for my mother. She'd never believe it."

I had to drop behind Norma to let a line of racers wearing those white plastic helmets like spacemen whip by us. I'll never know why people want to race through pretty scenery. What's the point of being in the woods if you don't have time to see a goldfinch looping across the path and watch the shadows play? Norma isn't much for nature, either. She goes biking for the exercise. Jen's the one who'll get as thrilled as I get at finding a patch of hepatica. That's pinky-sized flowers with hairy stems that bloom among dead leaves.

Jen got me interested in nature when we lived in Brooklyn and Grandma wouldn't let us out unless we stayed together. Jen and I would take the bus to Prospect Park, promising Grandma to be back before dark, of course. We kept a notebook to describe the bugs and birds and bushes we saw. Then we'd go to the library and try to identify them. Half the time we couldn't, because our descriptions didn't match what was in the books.

"Tomorrow," I said as I pulled up alongside Norma again, "you go tell Ms. Hawkins that I'm thinking of killing myself. Let's see if she sends me to Belloti."

"Sure thing," Norma said and offered me a piece of gum.

43

Pooh came out of his sulk in the van on the way home and insisted on doing elephant jokes with Norma and me. Question: Why does a two-ton elephant carry a trunk? Answer: Because she doesn't own a handbag. Norma and I even made up one of our own. What does a two-ton elephant say when it steps on your toe? Nothing, because elephants can't talk. I liked that well enough to try it out on my family at dinner that evening. Some sense of humor they have! Nobody laughed.

.  .  .

I couldn't believe how well the plan worked. Monday morning after Ms. Hawkins took attendance, Norma went up and whispered in her ear. Ms. Hawkins's dreamy smile disappeared and she gave me a sharp look. I stared straight ahead at the chalkboard, where someone had written an obscenity behind her back. Before I even got to see what Ms. Hawkins did about the obscenity, I was on my way to Mr. Belloti's office.

I had to sit outside his closed door waiting for him while the guidance office secretary typed away. A rainbow hung on the wall behind her head. It got a little boring to look at, and I was tempted to pick up a health magazine on the end table next to my chair. It had an article about baby fat, which is what Gerry says I have. Mother says I just eat too much. Anyway, I reached for the magazine but pulled back when I realized that a person who's thinking of killing herself isn't interested in her health.

Finally Mr. Belloti asked me to come into his office. He has the smallest office in the school, just big enough for two chairs and his desk. Lucky thing he's so skinny.

"So how are you doing, Casey?" He crossed one bony knee over the other and prepared for a long listen.

"Fine," I said, focusing on his saggy socks and trying hard to sound miserable.

"Any problems in school?"

"No."

"How about at home?"

"No problems."

"Lucky girl," he said pleasantly. "Most people have at least a problem or two. Would you say you're pretty happy, then?"

"Not really."

I let him coax it out of me, that my parents were separating and that they were separating my sister and me, too. When I got to the part about not being able to live without Jen, I didn't cry the way I normally would. I just shuddered. That seemed to impress Mr. Belloti a lot. He sent me back to my classroom, but first he got out my records and asked me if Mother's office number was still the same. That meant he was going to call her. I felt pretty hopeful, returning to class.

"Baloney, utter garbage. I don't believe it," Mother was raving as I dragged into the kitchen, head hanging, that evening. I'd gone to bed right after school and stayed there until Jen came into our room and asked me what my problem was. It was hard not to tell her, but I didn't, because I wasn't taking any chances of having her make me confess that I was acting.

"Case," Mother said. "What kind of baloney did you give that poor guy in the guidance office?"

"He's the school psychologist," I said virtuously. "I can't help it if my homeroom teacher sent me to see him."

"He says you're depressed and that . . . Case, you're putting on an act to get your own way, aren't you?" Mother said meanly.

"I don't know what you're talking about." I even managed to squeeze out a single wet tear, but Mother ignored it.

"Leave the child alone," Dad said. "You sound like a district attorney, Marian. Why shouldn't she be depressed, considering what's going on here?"

"You don't know this kid the way I do, Gerry."

"Oh, come on," he said. "I've known her over half her life."

I sighed pitifully and murmured, "I don't feel like eating. May I be excused, please?"

"You don't want to eat your dinner?" Mother said. "Are you sick?" She felt my forehead. "If this is a performance, I'm impressed."

I went off to bed proud enough at having shaken my mother to endure my hunger pangs. Now, what was next? I can't stand blood or violence. Drugs—but I'm not about to put anything into my body that might do weird things to me. Aspirin is the strongest drug I've ever taken because I've never been very sick. Aspirin. Suppose I swallowed a whole bottle of it. I didn't *think* it could kill me, but I wasn't sure. But if I didn't actually swallow any— just left the empty bottle around so they'd think I had—I could get rid of the tablets by flushing them down the toilet. And then what? Then they'd believe me. Maybe.

Good thing I hadn't confided in Jen. She'd never let me do anything this mean and rotten, but I couldn't be nice and keep the family together. Besides, Mother wasn't nice. I considered the matter of a note and decided to draw a broken heart, put Jen's name in one jagged half and my name in the other. That should be clear enough, even to Mother.

I would have to stay awake until they went to sleep, but my stomach hurt too much for that to be a problem.

A while later Jen came into the room and asked me how I was feeling.

"Bad," I said.

"Want me to bring you anything?"

I wanted to tell her that a hot roast-beef sandwich or even peanut butter and jelly would be great, but instead I sighed and said, "I wish I had something to read."

Jen sat down on the bed beside me. "Want me to read you *Charlotte's Web*?"

"Would you?" Jen read me the story of the wise and wonderful spider whenever I had a cold. It was one of our traditions, like the heart-shaped messages I sent her. But I thought of the pain I was going to cause her shortly and decided I didn't deserve the treat. "Maybe just a couple of pages, and then I'll close my eyes and try to sleep," I said.

Jen frowned at me. "Case, are you up to something?"

"Huh?" I tried to sound innocent, but Jen knows me too well.

"You're being awfully reasonable. When you're really sick, you're *never* reasonable.

"That's mean." I said. "Why are you being mean when I'm sick?"

"You *are* planning something. Tell me what you're up to."

I buried my head under my pillow so she couldn't read my face. "Go away. You don't have to read to me at all."

"Case, you're acting about three years old." Jen sounded disgusted.

"That's 'cause I'm sick," I said from under my pillow.

Silence. I waited. I'd never managed to fool Jen in my life. Well, I'd never really tried before. I don't know if she believed me or if she just decided to give up, but I came out from under my pillow when I heard the first lines of *Charlotte's Web*.

# ·SIX·

I WOKE UP SUDDENLY, startled to find I'd been asleep. Luckily, it was still dark, and the house was still quiet. So I hadn't missed my chance. Not that I was eager to do it, but I made myself tiptoe into the bathroom, empty the super-sized bottle of aspirin into the toilet and flush. Then I set out the big paper heart cut in jagged halves. Just to be sure they'd notice, I left the open bottle on the heart half with my name and put the toothpaste on the half that had Jen's name. Then I went back to bed and promptly fell asleep again.

The sun was up when they shook me awake. All three of them were standing around my bed yelling frantic questions at me. They looked as if they expected me to die any second. I concentrated on imitating a cooked noodle, figuring if I'd really swallowed those tablets, the least I'd be is limp.

Mother and Gerry fought over who was going to take me to the hospital and decided they both would. "She'll be all right. Don't worry," Mother told Jen and insisted Jen go to school. "You can call the hospital after your math test," Mother told her. I sure hoped Jen didn't fail.

They got me to the hospital emergency room before seven. I hadn't said a word. I sat between the parents on a plastic-covered couch, leaning against Gerry with my eyes closed.

Mother was babbling the way she does when she's nervous.

"Case isn't the kind of kid to hurt herself. She's dramatic, but not crazy enough to—she must be pretending. She wouldn't really—God, Gerry, do you think she really swallowed the whole bottle?"

"She could have."

"If she did, it's my fault. You think I'm a monster, don't you?" Mother said.

"Now who's being dramatic?" Gerry asked. "You don't take Case seriously, because she doesn't have the self-control you do, that's all."

"So I'm a lousy mother who doesn't understand her own kid."

"Not lousy," he said, "just a little hard-nosed."

I'd never heard Gerry being an authority on me to Mother before. It was weird. But then so was the whole situation. Finally, somebody with a high, sweet voice said, "Doctor's ready to see Case in the examining room now. And would one of you stay with me to fill out one last form, please?"

I kept my eyes closed and leaned heavily as Mother guided me from the waiting room, but I was squirming inside. I hate doctors' examinations. It's bad enough with our regular doctor, who's a woman, but now my body was going to get poked at by a stranger who'd probably be a man. Yuck! It was hard to stay noodley.

The doctor had a reassuring voice, but the first thing he did was scare me silly by sending my mother out of the room. I opened my eyes to find myself alone with a cute-looking guy with dimples who looked more like a college kid than a doctor, despite his white coat. I checked out his feet. Sure enough, running shoes. What kind of doctor wears running shoes? He was a fake, and my parents had left me in his power. I was lying on a squeaky sheet of paper on an examination table, a long jump from the floor. My impulse was to cut and run, but he smiled at me and said, "Seems there's a question about your dining on aspirin last night. How many did you take?"

49

I swallowed a few times and made noises like I was trying to talk, while he raised each of my eyelids and peered in with a pencil-sized flashlight. I hoped he couldn't tell much just by looking at me. "I took them all," I said, going for broke.

"Be too bad if you did. Nasty business having your stomach pumped." He stuck his tongue out and made a gagging sound. "I'd hate it myself," he said. "But we don't have any choice. If you really swallowed them all, we have to pump you out." He waited for me to beg for mercy. When I didn't, he said, "You're sure, now? No last-minute confession?"

I quivered in terror, but I'd come this far. Hadn't I claimed I'd do anything to save our family? I'd always wondered how brave I was. I was about to find out. I squeezed my eyes shut and crossed my hands on my chest, telling myself that if this didn't convince Mother that I was serious, nothing would.

Don't ever get your stomach pumped. A nurse stood beside me saying soothing things, but all those steely-looking instruments on the counters scared me, and nobody said which ones they were going to use on me, and then they came at me with this plastic tubing and stuck it up my nose. It was the grossest thing that's ever happened to me in my life. Besides, it hurt. They held me down so I couldn't get away, and I felt my guts being pulled up out of me. It was worse than the flu. It was awful and rotten and disgusting. When they were done, my parents came back in to collect my remains.

"Why did you go through with it, you crazy kid?" Gerry asked. "Why didn't you admit you hadn't swallowed anything?"

"How do you know?" I asked.

"Nothing in your stomach," Mother said. "Why'd you do it, Case?"

"So you'd believe me," I said. "It's not fair that you should get to do whatever you want and mow right over Jen and me. We should count even if we are kids. I want us to be a family forever, and I want to be together with my sister."

"And whenever you don't get your way, you're going to threaten to kill yourself?" my mother asked without any sympathy.

"Next time I won't threaten, I'll do it," I said wildly.

"Can you believe this kid? She's trying to hold us hostage," Mother said to Gerry. "You know something, Case? Your grandmother offered to have you and your sister come stay with her in Cincinnati. I'm so angry with you right now that I'm about ready to pack you off, but not with your sister—alone."

"Let's go home," Gerry said. "They want us out of here, and it's no place to quarrel." He sounded tired. "I'll take charge of Case, and you go to work, Marian. You don't want them to get the idea your family comes before your job. They might have second thoughts about promoting you, and there'd be no point in our separation then. Or would there be?"

"I'll go to work," Mother said. "And you stop letting Case manipulate you. She's no heroine, just a spoiled child who wants her own way."

"I think I'm capable of dealing with her without your help, thank you," he said.

"Are you? You were the one who believed her," Mother said.

"You believed me, too," I said.

"Only for a few foolish minutes. Never mind." Mother held up her hand. "I'm off. You think about your options, Case. Behave like a normal kid and do what your parents think best, or go live with Grandma."

"You're making your own mother sound like a bogeyman," Dad said.

"My mother *is* the bogeyman to Case."

We dropped Mother off at the train station so she could get the next train into New York City.

I had a big hole where my stomach had been, but when Gerry asked me if I was hungry, I said I couldn't eat anything yet. "Want to go down to the marina and check out *The Jokester* with

51

me? You could help me move my essentials onto it."

"You're moving onto the boat already? Why are you in such a rush?"

"Because it's less depressing to leave than to get left," he said. "I couldn't stand living in the house once your mother moved out."

I nodded, understanding how he felt. "Don't I have to go to school?" I thought to ask.

"Not unless you feel like it."

I said I felt more like checking out *The Jokester* with him, and squeezed his hand, grateful for his sympathy. I didn't blame him for refusing to let Mother push him around and make him move to a city he hated. I just wished he could have hung onto all of us instead of just me.

The air at the marina was warm, and sea gulls sailed through the blue sky like pointy white kites. I was glad not to be sitting in school stuffing my brain. In fact, I felt so good I began to get hungry. *The Jokester* is an old twin-diesel Hatteras that's basically a great boat, but it's no wonder nobody's bought it. Not only is it badly in need of a paint job, but its teak is splintery and gray and its metal parts look rusty.

"You can sit up on the fly bridge and enjoy the harbor until your stomach feels okay," Dad offered. I said I'd rather help him fill his stateroom drawers.

He'd done a neat job of organizing the stateroom with one bed for sleeping and the other made into a work space for his drawing board. "If only somebody buys my comic strips, I'll do okay here," he said when I complimented him. It didn't take much time to stow the clothes he'd brought from the house. All he'd taken so far were jeans and T-shirts.

"Want to see my latest masterpieces?" he asked.

"Sure." I hoped I'd know what to say about his work. He draws things about the future, like he had robots meeting for energy breaks instead of coffee breaks. In one strip two robots

52

are on an energy break trying to figure out why their boss had hired a worker who kept pressing the wrong buttons. They thought he should have hired the experienced person who applied for the job. In the last frame the boss is leering at the new worker, who's a sexy girl. One robot says, "It must be a glitch in his decision-making track," and the other robot agrees.

"Funny?" Gerry asked with a big smile.

"Oh, sure," I said to please him, but then I added honestly, "I guess it is if you have a thing for robots."

He sighed, and said, "Why don't you go check out the bow compartment, and see how it suits you."

"Any place would suit me fine if Jen was sharing it with me," I said.

"Tell me," he said. "Is your sister the only member of our family you love?"

"You know I love you a lot, Gerry. Besides being the only father I've ever had, you're excellent. Even Mother's not so bad most of the time. Of course, breaking up the family just so she can be a big shot is pretty obnoxious, but—"

"To be fair," he said, interrupting me, "it's not just your mother's career that's causing us trouble. It's an attitude she has that she can't help. She doesn't respect me, Case, and if I put up with the way she treats me, pretty soon I won't respect myself."

"What do you mean, she doesn't respect you? How do you know?"

"By the way she treats me."

"She treats everbody bad," I said. "You could work something out if you wanted."

"You're mad at me, too, a little, aren't you?" he said. "You think I deserve to stay alone on this boat with nobody to talk to or share meals with?"

"You could get a dog. Mother never let us have one, but you could get one now."

"A dog does not exactly fill the bill. A daughter is what I need."

"I can't help it," I yelled, bursting all of a sudden. "My sister is . . . the other half of my heart."

He put his arm around me and leaned his chin on my head while I sobbed. Mother would have been disgusted with me, but not Gerry. I should have appreciated that, but, instead, when I could talk, I suggested, "Couldn't you find a place on land you could afford so Jen and I could both keep you company? Maybe Mother could chip in to help you support us?"

"That does it," he said, and jerked away from me.

I'd landed with both left feet on his sore ego. All I could think of to show I did care about him was to go to work on the smelly refrigerator with a pail of cold water and Boat Zoap. It was a sickening job, and when I was through and we were ready to leave, he just said, "Thanks, kid." I'd really hurt him a lot.

. . .

That evening I was at Norma's house, sharing Pooh's birthday dinner. While I was helping Norma and her mother do the dishes, I told Norma what had happened to me at the hospital.

"And the worst of it was," I said, "that Mother wasn't impressed at all once she realized I hadn't actually done anything to myself. So I'm back to square one. And now Gerry's acting pitiful about me not wanting to keep him company on the boat. He's making me feel so guilty."

"Did your stepfather ever formally adopt you?" Norma's mother asked.

I'd almost forgotten she was listening. She doesn't usually butt in between Norma and me. "Not as far as I know," I said. "Why?"

"He loves Case and Jen just like they're his own kids," Norma said. "What's he need to adopt them for?"

"Legal reasons," Norma's mother said. "For instance, if Case's mother and he get divorced, he's no relation to Case at all anymore. I'm surprised that her mother's sending her to live with him. You're sure he never legally adopted you, Case?''

"Not as far as I know," I answered. "But I'll ask Mother."

Pooh liked my present better than anything else he got. Norma was jealous. "I spent three weeks' allowance to get him a model car, and you give him stickers and he's thrilled to pieces. It's not fair!"

"Remember my hat with the false teeth that you gave me, and Jen was insulted because I said it was my favorite present?" I asked Norma.

Norma smiled. "That was the first year we were best friends. I was scared you'd think my present was stupid, but I didn't have enough money to get anything nice. Oh, Case, don't go live with your grandma. Please!" Norma never got teary, but she looked so close to crying that I hugged her.

"Something will work out. You'll see," I said. But I wasn't so sure anymore.

My mother was doing bills at her desk in the living room when I got home from Norma's. Gerry was watching TV, and Jen wasn't downstairs.

"Mother," I said, stepping behind her and leaning on the back of her chair. "How come Gerry never adopted Jen and me?"

"What makes you ask that question?"

"Norma's mother thinks it's funny that you're sending me to live on the boat with Gerry when he's not my real father, and if you got divorced he wouldn't even be my stepfather anymore, she says."

"I told you separation is not divorce. This is just a temporary arrangement. . . . Anyway, Norma's mother should mind her own business."

"She does. She just happened to be there when I was talking to Norma. Norma's mother's a really nice lady."

"You think everybody's nice except your own mother."

"Well, you haven't *been* very nice lately."

55

"You and I have always had a hard time getting along," Mother said. "Gerry thinks it's because we're alike. Do you see yourself as like me?"

I certainly did not. "I wouldn't act like you," I said. "I'd know my kids had feelings, and I'd be kind to them."

"So I'm not kind?"

"Not to me," I said.

Mother sniffed. "Believe it or not, I've tried to be. I've tried very hard, but now I'm determined to be kind to myself. For the first time in my life, I'm getting some recognition." She looked at me over her shoulder for a second and then told me quietly to sit down.

I promptly dragged a footstool over and sat hugging my knees. Heart-to-heart talks with Mother were rare, and I sensed one coming.

"All right," she began. "I don't know if you're old enough to understand, but it's time I tried to make you see my point of view. Here goes with your mother's official autobiography. . . .

"I got married before I should have and became a mother before I ever had a chance to find out where my capabilities lay. My husband got leukemia and died, leaving me a young widow with outrageous medical bills to pay off, and not one but two kids to support. Well, I worked and went to school nights trying to dig myself out of that hole. Your grandma was a reluctant baby-sitter. She'd never much liked little children. She only did it because she'd been the one who kept urging me to use my brains to get somewhere in life.

"So I managed, but then I met Gerry, and he was sweet and fun to be with and great with you girls. I didn't want another husband, especially not an unambitious one like him, who didn't appear to be going anywhere in life. But he hung around, and I grew fond of him. He claimed he understood that I was ambitious, and would support my career. He said you kids needed a father. And you girls were obviously crazy about him. I worried because he's younger than I am, and too soft a man for me, but—anyway, I married him. And it worked all right for a while.

"He wanted to adopt you, Case, you and Jen both, but especially you. He adores you, but I kept putting him off. I guess I didn't want him to have any stronger hold on us than he already had."

"So you were always going to divorce him," I accused.

"I always had reservations, but he knew that when he married me."

"*I* didn't know," I said. "I thought we had a family, a real one that was going to last."

"It may still," she said. "I keep telling you this is only temporary. I don't know how much I'm going to miss him, Case. He makes me furious sometimes, but I'm still attached to him. You'll have to be patient and let me work things out."

"*You're* not patient. Why should I be?"

"Look, Case, you have a choice. You don't have to stay with Gerry. You can come with Jen and me, and we'll try you out in the public school for the rest of this term, and if that doesn't work—"

"No, thanks," I said. "I'll stick by Gerry. Somebody has to be loyal to him."

Mother got that stiff look that meant I'd hurt her, but I didn't care. Gerry might not be a superachiever, but he loved me a lot, and, besides, he was the only father I'd ever known. I left Mother, feeling worse than when I'd had my stomach pumped, and went upstairs to find Jen.

She was lying on her bed staring again. "Jen, what are we going to do?" I cried.

Jen's eyes were dark and mysterious in the lamplight. "You always think something can be done," she said sadly.

"Of course something can be done. Something can always be done."

"What?" Jen asked.

57

I didn't know. I felt so frustrated—a kid being done to again. All I could do back was yell and stamp my feet. Well, I'd yell if nothing else. "They can't have it all their way," I yelled. "It's not right."

"Oh, Case, I'm going to miss you so much," Jen said. "I'm older, but you do the fighting, and I let you even when it's my battle, too, because I hate fighting and you're braver than me."

We hugged each other for a while, and then I told her what was really scaring me. "If we're not together, Jen, will we still be close?"

"Nobody can change how we feel about each other. We'll always be close," she said.

"Except that I'm going to be living on the boat with Dad, and you're going to be living in New York City with Mother."

I knew she hadn't been talking about physical distance, but she didn't bother to correct me. Instead, she said, "Remember when we went to the Museum of Natural History together?"

"Not too well. I was only a baby."

"Right. Now we can go again easily. You'll come to stay for the weekend, and we'll do all kinds of things together in the city. It'll be fun. And we'll have so much to tell each other. . . ."

"But I haven't gotten my period yet," I yelled in desperation. "Who's going to be there when I get my period? Not even Mother will be there."

"You'll manage," Jen said. "We both will, somehow."

# ·SEVEN·

YOU'D THINK WORRYING WOULD have some use, considering how much of it people do. But it doesn't. If things turn out better than you expect, you've made yourself miserable for nothing, and if they turn out worse, well, who needs an early start on suffering? It was worse for me when Jen and Mother moved to New York City and Gerry and I moved onto the boat. I felt homesick for Jen and our house and even for Mother a little. Nights were bad, especially. Even though I took my ancient teddy, Bearheart, to bed with me, I kept looking at the bow bunk across from mine and wishing Jen were in it. I tried filling that bunk up with schoolbooks, the art projects my teacher kept making us take home, dirty clothes and miscellaneous junk, but it still looked like a black hole to me.

I thought Jen must be missing me, too, but on my first weekend visit to Mother's little apartment, I asked Jen if it wasn't rough adjusting to a new school so late in the term.

She sounded apologetic when she told me, "Not really." Then she added, "And the computer stuff they're doing is so sophisticated—I can't believe it! . . . How are you making out, Case?"

"Okay," I said. I didn't want her feeling sorry for me, at least not as sorry as I was feeling for myself. "It's fun living on a boat. The gulls and the ducks are right there, and people are so friendly. Nobody cares about clothes or time, and cleaning up is a cinch. I bet you'd like it, Jen."

"If I didn't have to live on motion-sickness medicine, I might."

I tried another tack. "You know, that pregnant lady didn't get the mortgage; so our house is still for sale. We could move back to it, just you and me, until it's sold."

"I really like the school I'm in, Case," Jen said carefully. "Anyway, the house will sell soon, I bet."

"Oh, sure," I said. "I know. I wasn't serious."

I thought of the awful moment when Mrs. Delaney had brought the pregnant lady into my bedroom while I was packing.

"I suppose this room could be the nursery," the lady had said, opening my closet door as if she already owned it.

"It's a very solid house," Mrs. Delaney said and winked at me. She'd thought it was funny when she'd called Mother up about the house problems, and Mother had made me call Mrs. Delaney back and confess how I'd tricked her.

I hadn't said a word to the pregnant lady, just kept packing my sewing basket, my red stick-on paper for making hearts and the Russian tea tin with my baby tooth and locks of hair from Jen and me. After Mrs. Delaney and her client had left the room, I'd carved Jen's name and mine just above the doorknob where nobody would notice: "Jen and Case, their room."

Every evening I called Jen from the bank of telephones outside the shed where small boats were stored in the winter. One night I came back from briefing Jen on my day's happenings and found Gerry trying out keys in the lock of the box on the bow that held *The Jokester*'s spare lines. He stopped whistling to give me a big smile when I squatted next to him.

"Beautiful evening, isn't it?" he asked.

"I forgot to tell Jen what my math teacher did to me today," I moaned.

"So tell *me*," he said.

I sighed. As far as his reactions went whenever I told him about my school day, I might as well have been talking in Swahili.

60

Also, if I happened to catch him at his drawing board, forget it. He wouldn't hear a thing. "How come you're so cheerful?" I accused him. "I thought you'd be sad and lonely without Mother and Jen."

"Well, I am sometimes," he said, "but I like what I'm doing now; so I'm not as miserable as I expected. Sorry, Case. . . . Are you going to tell me what your math teacher did to you, or not?"

"He reduced me a whole grade for forgetting to put my name on the paper."

"Um."

"Well, isn't that mean and rotten?"

"He ought to be shot," Dad said, and grinned as if he expected me to be pleased.

I tried again. "Norma nominated me for the planning committee for the field-day activities, but I wasn't elected."

When I'd told Jen that, she'd said it was mean and that I'd have made a great field-day-activity committee person, but Gerry said, "Lucky you. Now you can enjoy the field day without being responsible for its success."

"What kind of attitude is that?" I demanded. "Mother would never say a thing like that. It's—it's anti-American."

"Is it? Well, being responsible for things has never struck me as a pleasure. Maybe at heart I'm a bum. Now tell me, Case, why aren't you happy on this boat with me?"

"I need to be a whole family," I said.

"I kind of thought it'd be easier for you without your mother bugging you for a while," he said.

"Easier isn't necessarily better."

"You've got a point there," he said. "A good one. All right. But, Case, I don't see being a whole family as happening again soon. You've got to adjust to that." He kept on talking, but I wasn't listening. I was wondering how long separations lasted before they turned into divorce.

"My big problem is money," he was saying when I tuned in again. "If somebody doesn't buy the house soon, and I don't sell any cartoons, I'm going to have to get some part-time work. . . . What do you think of a teak repair and refinishing service for boatmen?"

"It took you a whole week to do the rail around the aft deck," I pointed out.

"I had a lot of interruptions," he said. Then he asked me straight out, "Do you think your stepfather's a bum, Case?"

"Of course not." I gave him a hug and said, "I think you're excellent." Really, I didn't want him to feel bad, just not to be so comfortable being separated.

Gerry talked to lots of people at the marina, but the one I noticed him talking to most was Miki. She'd bounced over to the boat one Saturday when he was working on the teak and said, "Boy, could I use someone like you." In two minutes she'd told him all about the sailboat she and her brother had bought cheap. Next thing I knew he'd gone off to look it over.

He was gone so long, I'd had to walk to the train station to pick up Jen by myself. After that, either he was with Miki, or Miki was around *The Jokester*. She was pretty cute and had a neat figure that she was always showing off in tight T-shirts and shorts, but I didn't worry, because I figured she was paying him to work on her boat.

"Does Miki have a lot of money?" I asked him one day.

"Nursery-school teachers don't make much," he said.

"Then is her brother paying you for helping with their boat?"

"Not really," he said. "Mainly I'm just acting as a consultant. Their boat's in pretty bad shape, and if they want to use it this summer—"

"Can't her brother help her?"

"He doesn't live around here. I like helping Miki. She's a really nice kid."

"Kid?"

"Well, she's only twenty-two or -three. To a fellow pushing forty like me, she's a kid."

"You're not pushing forty; you're thirty-seven. Mother's the one who's forty."

"Unfortunately. That's why she's so set on this promotion. She's sure it's the last chance she'll have."

"You could still do your cartoons in an apartment in New York, Dad."

"Come on, Case, I told you how I feel about being your mother's dependent. Besides, I'm still convinced that she's wrong about life. It should be a mixed bag, with time for family and friends and work and fooling around and even just taking it easy, not a marathon race."

"We were good together for four whole years," I said. "Why's everybody changing except me? Jen even joined a computer club. She always hated clubs. She says she misses me, but she sounds happy enough."

"Case," he said, "aren't you glad that Jen's finally fitting in with kids her own age?"

I gave up talking heart-to-heart with him after that. He just didn't understand.

Norma wasn't a whole lot of help, either. I kept inviting her down to the boat, but her interest in boats has a minus sign after it. Her big thing was the vegetable garden she and her brother were planting. I went over to help with it, but I wore out fast chopping up clods of dirt and ended up in the house talking to Norma's mother. She was quilting, which looked more like fun than farming. I considered making a small quilt for Jen's birthday. Norma's mother offered to help me, but she isn't a chatty lady, and she kept right on watching a TV show when she wasn't putting a stitch in the quilt. I went back to the marina early.

I know it's disgusting to feel sorry for yourself, but what could I do? I was walking around with this soggy lump in my chest, and I didn't know how to get rid of it. That's what I was thinking

63

about when I slammed into Brian right on our dock. He's the nicest of the dock persons the marina hires to help boatmen in and out of their slips.

"What're you daydreaming about, Case?" he asked.

"I'm not daydreaming. I'm suffering," I blurted out.

"About what?"

"About everything. I want things to be the way they were, but nobody else does."

He thought about it. He's kind of freckled and cute with narrow blue eyes. "Life wouldn't be too interesting if nothing changed," he said. Then he told me he'd be glad to talk about it sometime, but he had a drunk captain bringing a boat in, and the guy might smash into the pilings again if Brian wasn't there to help. He gave me a wink and hurried off.

. . .

If Dad wasn't on our boat, he was usually on Miki's. Evenings he'd come back to *The Jokester* so that I wouldn't be alone. Then he and Miki would sit around drinking beer and talking and laughing and watching what they could see of the sunset together. They didn't exactly exclude me, but they didn't invite me into their conversation, either. We had a little TV in the saloon, and I spent a lot of time watching it. Or else I'd walk up the dock to call Jen. Dad still hadn't installed a phone on the boat. That annoyed Mother. She said she'd offered to pay for one because there should be a phone in case somebody got sick.

"It makes him feel bad when you offer to pay," I tried to explain to Mother.

"Don't be ridiculous, Case," my mother said. "I can afford it, and he can't."

I was beginning to understand why Dad wanted to be separated, but Mother obviously didn't yet.

Brian was becoming sort of a friend of mine. He usually stopped to talk to me, and he taught me things about boats, like how to grab a line and make it fast when a boat was coming into a slip or tying up to the gas dock. I was quick with knots, he said. I wondered if Jen would think Brian was cute. He'd caught a glimpse of her when she visited me and asked me who she was. "Pretty," he'd said. "Is she a college girl?"

"Not yet," I'd said, and didn't tell him she was only fourteen. If she liked him, she might want to hang around the marina with me more this summer. They already had something in common. I knew because Brian and I had been talking about the sailboats that never left their slips, and I'd said, "If I had a sailboat, I'd be out on the sound all the time."

"Me, too," he'd answered and asked immediately, "Does your sister like sailing?"

"Jen loves computers." I'd said that because I didn't want to discourage him by saying no.

"Really!" he'd said. "That's my main interest. You've got to get me together with that sister of yours next time she comes."

"Saturday," I'd promised.

But I wasn't going to introduce them until I'd had a chance to really talk to Jen myself. Three-minute nightly phone calls—Mother actually made Jen use a timer—just weren't enough to give me the full picture of how the separation was going at their end. And I wanted to warn my sister that our family was sliding right into a divorce, even if nobody else could see it but me.

. . .

The sky was bulging with huge dark clouds when I got home from school Thursday afternoon, but I kind of like summer storms, and the marina's an exciting place to watch one from. Halyards clinked like cymbals in a rhythm band against the metal masts of the sailboats as the wind whooshed by. Even the inner harbor, where it's usually calm, had mean little tweaky waves. All the boats were in, of course, and they were heaving and rocking and rolling in their slips. When I got to *The Jokester,* I found Miki and Gerry sitting side-by-side on the aft deck studying a chart.

"Boy, we're going to have some storm," I said. "What're

65

you guys doing?''

"Dreaming," Miki said promptly. "We're charting a course to the Bahamas with some maps I found on my boat."

"Really," I said, hoping it was just dreaming and not something Gerry might up and do. I went down to the galley for milk and date-nut bread, but the bread was all gone. Gerry has as bad a sweet tooth as I do. I thought about the ice-cream dispenser on the dock and figured I might just make it there and back before the storm broke.

"I'm going to see if they refilled the ice-cream machine," I told them on my way back off the boat. They barely looked up from their chart. I didn't at all like the way his arm was draped along the back of her chair.

I walked up the swaying wooden ramp, which was missing half the crosspieces that keep your feet from sliding, thinking that if the marina was this full of motion when Jen came Saturday, she'd get seasick before she even got to *The Jokester*. Below me a small Chris Craft was bucking in its slip like a horse in a rodeo. Its bow lines were loose, and it looked ready to slam into the dock. There wasn't a person in sight, and it was a long way to the dockmaster's office. I decided I'd tighten the lines myself.

It wasn't as easy as I'd expected. I had hold of the bow line and was trying to hitch it onto the post, but I nearly got yanked off the dock instead when the boat heaved up away from me. I grabbed for a post and was holding onto it with one arm while I held the line in my other hand and one of my legs dangled over the water. It was scary, and I nearly had a heart attack when somebody grabbed me from behind.

"Case! What are you trying to do to yourself?" my father yelled into my ear. He took the line away from me and got it tied fast. I tried to help him with the other bow line, but he nearly snapped my head off. "Wait right there."

"What are you so mad about?" I asked him when he was finished taming the Chris Craft.

66

"If Miki hadn't decided she wanted some ice cream, too"— he looked at me bleakly—"you could have crushed a leg or an arm or worse. Why did you endanger yourself like that?"

I didn't say anything, just shrugged.

"Did you think that if you got hurt your mother and sister would take care of you?"

"I'm not that crazy," I said indignantly. "I was just trying to be helpful to Brian, and the boat was stronger than I thought."

"I wonder," he said, giving me the eye as if he didn't believe me.

I would have told him that I'd changed and wasn't the silly kid who got her stomach pumped anymore if I hadn't been so occupied with finding that interesting fact out myself. I still wanted to keep the family together, but now I knew far-out tricks wouldn't do that.

"What kind of ice cream does Miki want?" I asked and took the money from him and went back up the ramp. On my way to the machines, I stopped at the phone booths and took a trembly whiff of salt air. I felt so low that I needed to talk to Jen.

It was Mother who answered the phone. "How come you're home so early?" I asked.

"Sick," Mother croaked. "Sore throat. Home in bed all day."

"You must be dying," I said. Mother never stayed home from work for anything.

"101," Mother said proudly. "Your sister's not home yet. She's due any minute."

Mother took the telephone number of my pay phone. I said I hoped she'd feel better and offered to get on the next train to the city if she needed me to come and nurse her.

"No, thanks, love, I'll be fine tomorrow," Mother said. She sounded pleased that I'd offered, which gave me a guilty twinge because I only wanted to come for my own sake, really.

I sat down in the lee of a large metal trash bin at the end of a floating finger dock near enough to hear the phone ring when

Jen called. A gull was balancing in the wind. It was trying to land on the bow of a big cruiser, but the wind was so strong it couldn't get down. The gull slid sideways on outstretched wings and flew off to try its luck somewhere else. Empty oil cans were rolling around under the huge hoist that was big enough to lift sixty-foot boats up out of the water for repairs. The cans clanged so loudly that I almost didn't hear the telephone ring. I leaped to grab the receiver.

"How's it going, Case?" Jen asked.

"Well,"—I rushed to jam it all in before the timer went off— "I can't wait till I see you, but it's good you're not here today, because the weather's rotten, and I nearly got my leg crushed by a boat, and Dad thought I did it on purpose, but I'm not that stupid anymore. And Brian wants to meet you when you come Saturday. I'm sure you'll like him, and he loves computers, too."

"Case, what are you up to? You know I can't talk to boys." I could almost see Jen blushing over the phone.

"Don't worry. He'll do all the talking," I said. "Anyway, that's not the important thing. Something's going on here that I need your help with."

"What?"

"I haven't got time to tell you. You'll see when you get here."

"Okay. Listen, Case, Mother wants you to meet us downtown the Saturday after this one to go shopping for some summer clothes for us."

"Oh, fun! Ask her if she'll take us out to lunch, and then can I stay overnight at the apartment and Sunday you and I can go to the Bronx Zoo? Remember we talked about how you could take me to the zoo now?"

"Well, but not that Sunday. See, there's an orientation meeting for a computer camp I could be going to, and my teacher wants me to attend."

"A computer camp? How long are you going for?"

"Well, it depends," Jen said evasively. "It's expensive, but

68

my teacher says he could get me a scholarship because another student of his that was supposed to go, can't. So—Case, this is the most incredible thing that's ever happened to me. I'm hoping you'll understand. . . .''

"Understand what?" I asked. "You're going to spend the summer with me, aren't you?"

"Case, don't sound that way. We'll talk about it Saturday," Jen said, and hung up because the timer was buzzing.

I leaned my head against the cool glass of the booth door waiting to cry, but nothing came. The soggy lump just spread in my chest.

That night Gerry and I went to a pizza parlor together, just the two of us. I felt good having him all to myself for a change. When I'd finished the last crust of my last slice of pizza with mushrooms and green peppers, I asked him, "Are you falling in love with Miki?"

"You don't have to worry, Case," he said. "Miki's just a friend."

"You're sure?" I asked.

"Listen," he said. "There's only one thing I like better about Miki than your mother."

"What's that?" I asked, thinking I knew—her looks.

"Miki believes in me," Gerry said.

That surprised me without especially relieving me, because it was even worse. More important than looks. I wondered if Mother'd care if she knew how he felt. Maybe I could get Jen to tell her. Saturday I had better have a talk with Jen.

# ·EIGHT·

I TRIED TO GREET Jen with something special when it was her turn to come to me because I knew that besides hating the boat, she hated getting up at dawn to make the early-morning train out of Grand Central. That was the train I made her take so we'd have most of Saturday together. Today I had a paper chain cut out of red hearts with a big black letter on each spelling out "Welcome Jen." I counted on her being more pleased than embarrassed if people stared at us when I fanned out the hearts.

She looked so pretty when she climbed off the train. Her cheeks were pink because people *were* staring and smiling, but also she looked older to me. I didn't know if she'd changed suddenly, or if I just hadn't noticed when I saw her every day. Anyway, I gave her a hug and a pinch to make sure she was really there.

"Ouch, Case, that hurts, You're so brown. You look as if you've been on vacation already."

"I do my homework up on the fly bridge after school, and I'm outside a lot. Brian can't wait to meet you. He'll be on duty this afternoon; so you can't duck out."

"I came to see *you*, not some stupid college boy," Jen said. She fingered the hearts, smiling, then tucked them carefully into her purse. I insisted on carrying her backpack for her.

"Do you have to bring so many books?" I asked as I got my arms adjusted through the straps and hefted the pack onto my back.

"I have to keep up with all the work they give me."

"But the term's practically over, and your math teacher already thinks you're a genius. Don't waste time on homework, Jen. I have so much to tell you."

"Even you can't talk nonstop for a whole weekend," Jen said, smiling at me. "Now what were you being so mysterious about on the phone?"

"You'll see."

"No, tell me so I'm prepared."

"Well, I'd rather see if you see the same thing I see," I said.

We walked down the stairs and started through the dingy streets toward the marina. Sweat tickled down my spine. It was hot. Gerry had offered to drive me, but I'd wanted Jen all to myself. Besides, he was busy scraping paint off the stern of *The Jokester,* and the scaffolding he'd rigged was tricky for him to get on and off of.

"Is it about Gerry?" Jen asked.

"And Miki," I said, and blurted the whole thing out. Suspense is not my thing. "She keeps touching him and leaning like—I think she'd like to be his girlfriend."

"I'm not surprised," Jen said. "Usually when people separate they find someone to take the place of their spouse pretty quickly."

"Their spouse?" I repeated. I knew what the word meant, but it didn't sound like Jen.

"I got a book out of the library on separation and divorce," Jen said.

"You did?" I was impressed. I didn't even know there were books on the subject. A dreadful thought struck me. "*Mother* doesn't have a boyfriend?"

"I don't think so. She hasn't got time. She works late every night and brings more home besides. She's not getting along with her boss, and you saw how terrible she looks."

"You must be lonesome."

71

"Not really. I stay after school a lot. The other computer kids do, too, and we talk. . . . I miss you, Case, but actually, with all the schoolwork and staying late and then splitting the chores around the apartment with Mother, I'm so busy that I don't have time to think about being lonely."

"But it would still be better if we all lived together again, wouldn't it?" I asked.

"Sure, at least you could do the cooking then," Jen said. She was trying to be funny. Neither Mother nor she liked cooking.

As we passed the boat repair hangar and headed toward *The Jokester*'s slip, Jen said, "Miki seems like she'd be easy to get along with."

"Jen!" I was shocked. "Even if she were the best person in the world, I wouldn't want her as my mother. I mean, Mother could be nicer and tell me what a terrific kid I am, but at least she's solid. How'd you like to spend your whole life learning to live with a mama bear and find yourself dealing with a bunny rabbit instead?"

"I wish I could tell Mother you said that," Jen said.

"What for?"

"Because she thinks you hate her."

"Me? She's the one doesn't like me," I said, but then I had to add, honestly, "—most of the time. Sometimes I do hate her. . . . Are you going to tell her about Miki wanting to be Dad's girlfriend?"

"Of course not!" Jen sounded shocked. "That's Dad's business. He has to be the one to say something like that."

"How about just telling her what Dad said about Miki? It's important, Jen. If Mother understood what's really bothering him, it could make all the difference."

"What did he say?"

"That Miki believes in him. He doesn't think Mother does."

Jen thought about it. "I can't tell Mother that. It's the same thing as telling her she's got competition."

72

"But shouldn't she know if she does?"

"I don't think she'll care," Jen said sorrowfully. "She wouldn't have moved to New York and left him behind if she cared about losing him."

"They're going to end up divorced, aren't they?" I said.

"They may, except that Mother's not very happy right now. Maybe she'll decide the job's not worth it."

And maybe I could help her decide, I thought, but I didn't discuss that with Jen. She'd be sure to say I shouldn't meddle.

Miki was standing on the floating finger talking to Gerry as he worked. I nudged Jen to notice that Miki had on platform heels with her tight shorts to make her legs look sexier. Jen raised her eyebrows and nodded.

"Jen!" Gerry yelled. "How's my girl?" He waved the paint scraper at us and stood up, balancing carefully as he climbed onto the deck of the boat to give Jen a kiss. He transferred some paint flakes from his face to hers, which gave us all something to laugh about.

"What's new in the Big Apple?" Miki asked. "I'll bet you could fry eggs on the sidewalk there this morning."

"It's hot," Jen said.

"Jen doesn't mind the heat," I said.

"Your little sister thinks you can walk on water," Miki said.

Dad broke the silence by asking, "Anyone ready for a snack?"

"I guess so," Jen said. "I am, anyway."

"Why don't you girls stow Jen's things while Gerry and I whip up something fantastic in the galley—like peanut butter on crackers. Okay?" Miki said.

I wondered who'd invited her to be hostess, but I knew better than to ask, considering the satisfied grin on Gerry's face. "Maybe I'll show Jen the English sailboat," I said.

When we were out of earshot, Jen said she wasn't very interested in sailboats, even ones that had crossed the Atlantic, and why didn't we go get a soda from the machine instead.

73

"Okay," I agreed. "She's a lot prettier than Mother, isn't she?"

"Don't worry so much, Case. They have to lead their own lives, and they won't listen to you, anyway."

"Mother might listen to you," I said.

"Miki's probably a very nice person."

"Big deal," I said. "Who wants nice around all the time?"

"Maybe Gerry does."

"I'm going to tell Mother if you don't."

"No, you're not," Jen said. "You keep out of their business. If it gets serious, he'll tell her."

"But then it'll be too late. Adults are disgusting," I said. "They're selfish. And I'm tired of being treated as if I don't matter. Don't they understand that what they do changes our lives, too? Don't we count for *anything*?"

"When you're an adult, you'll probably treat your kids the same way—if you have any," Jen said.

"Never," I told her.

Lunch was a tuna-fish salad. I'd pigged out on the peanut-butter crackers and was too full to eat much salad. Dad talked about how Buddy was glad to have him do all the work on the boat but very slow to send money to cover the supplies Dad needed. Finally he asked Jen how school was, but when Jen just said, "Good," he let it go at that. You'd think he'd know by now that you need to ask her specific questions if you really want answers. She's not only shy, she also doesn't expect people to be interested in her life.

"I had a terrible time in high school," Miki offered. "I was so shy, I didn't talk to anybody except the same friends I'd had since elementary school. I never even dated until I got to college."

"No kidding?" Gerry said. "I would have pegged you for most popular kid in the class."

"Oh, not me," Miki said. "I wanted to go out for cheerleading, but I was too self-conscious. It took college to get me out of myself. It's hard to be a teenager. Don't you think so, Jen?"

"So far," Jen said.

"And you look so mature," Miki said. "I'll bet people expect more of you because you look older than you are."

Jen looked at her as if she thought Miki was a mind reader. "I used to stutter," Jen said. "Sometimes if a boy talks to me and I don't know how to answer, I'm afraid I'm going to stutter again."

Miki nodded sympathetically. Gerry looked impressed. Now what? Was Miki going to win Jen over? Brian asked for permission to come aboard just then, and I was so glad to have him interrupting that I answered for Gerry, "Sure, Brian. Come on."

Brian stepped up onto the aft deck. We were eating there to catch any air movement resembling a breeze.

"Want a dab of tuna fish, Brian?" Gerry asked, pointing a fork at the bowl on the table.

"No, thanks. I've just finished lunch. I came to meet the computer whiz and to deliver a message to Miki. Your brother's aboard your boat and looking for you." Brian smiled at me.

"No kidding?" Miki said. "He wasn't supposed to show today. Excuse me, folks. I have to run." She stopped at the top of the ramp, made a megaphone with her hands and called, "Have a nice day, Jen." Then she raced off. I wondered if she really ever had been shy in high school. She sure didn't act it now.

Gerry said he'd better get back to work, and I offered to clean up the lunch things. That left Brian and Jen more or less alone. She looked scared, but I figured Brian could handle it and refused Jen's offer to help in the galley.

In about fifteen minutes, I had the dishes washed and put away and returned aft to find I'd been right. Brian and Jen were babbling on about Basic and Logo and Fortran, which I know are computer languages, but I still couldn't translate what they were saying into plain English.

It was really too humid for sunbathing, but I stretched out on

75

some flotation cushions so I could be close to them in case they said anything interesting. It was nice they were getting along so well, but I was impatient for Brian to leave so I'd have Jen to myself again. They kept talking, and soon the heat and a full stomach made me doze off. When I woke up, Gerry was whistling as he scraped away on the stern. Nobody else was around. "Where'd they go?" I asked him.

"Brian had to get down to the gas dock and asked your sister to go along. At the rate they were going, they'll be talking all afternoon. I've never heard Jen say so much at one time before."

"She talks," I said.

"I know she does to you, honey. You bring out the talker in people."

"Is that good?" I asked.

"I'd say so. Have I told you recently how glad I am to have you aboard?"

"Really?" It had seemed to me he barely noticed me, now he had Miki for company.

"Really," he assured me warmly.

Then I pushed it too far and asked, "Would you rather be with me or Miki?"

"Now, Case, play fair," he said. "You'd rather be with friends your own age than with your parents most of the time, wouldn't you?"

"Most of the time I'd rather be with Jen," I said, and shrugged and let it go. "I'm going after her. I wanted Brian to meet her, not hog her company."

Gerry grunted, and I took off. Would I rather be with Norma or my parents? It depended on what mood I was in and what problems I had. More important right now was being with Jen. She was leaving around four Sunday so she'd get home before evening when Mother said the subways were dangerous. That left us only twenty-six more hours together.

"I'm hoping to go to computer camp this summer," Jen was

76

saying to Brian, who had the gas hose in a humongous twin-diesel cabin cruiser. "That's if I get accepted and they give me a scholarship for the whole six weeks."

"Six weeks!" My screech made the gulls on the stanchions take off and the crabby-faced captain of the cruiser stare down at me. "Jen, I was counting on your spending the summer with me. Six weeks?"

"Calm down, Case," Brian said. "You'll still have me."

"So what? You're not my sister," I said. I was so upset I didn't care about whose feelings I hurt.

"I'd make a good substitute brother, wouldn't I?" he asked.

"No, you wouldn't," I said angrily. He was treating me like a little kid, showing off for Jen and acting big. "A substitute brother who likes you a little can't take the place of a real sister who loves you." It was one of those lucky moments when the right words came on time. I turned around and marched back to *The Jokester,* expecting Jen to follow me, but she didn't.

"What's the matter with you?" Gerry asked me when I stomped onto the boat. He was sitting there drinking a beer, finished with his scraping.

"I hate everybody," I said, and went down to my bow bunk and pushed Jen's backpack off it so that I could curl up and stare out the porthole at the gull on the post in the water.

It seemed to take forever until Jen got there. She sat down on the other bunk and said, "Case, I'm sorry. Listen, I won't go to computer camp. Even if I get in, I won't go. I'd rather be with you."

"No, you wouldn't. You hate the boat, and you'd have to keep taking stuff so you wouldn't be seasick all the time. But, at least, you could help me stop Miki from stealing Dad."

"Case," Jen said, "we can't do that. Dad's going to change, and Mother's changing, and you and I are changing, too."

"Not me. I'm not," I assured her. Then I remembered that I'd had the same thought recently.

"You are changing," Jen said. "And pretty soon you won't need me anymore. Not the way you do now, anyhow."

"I'll never not need you," I said.

"All right. Don't get all worked up about it. I'll go to computer camp some other year. This summer I'll spend as much time as I can with you."

"Why? Because you feel sorry for me?" I asked.

"No, because you matter most to me."

That was what I wanted to hear. It made me my old cheerful self through the whole rest of the day, and I didn't even complain about Gerry's eating more than his fair share of the popcorn at the movie he took us to see that evening.

"Having fun, honey?" he asked my on the way home.

"Sure I am," I said, "now that Jen's here."

# ·NINE·

ALL THE WAY TO the phone Tuesday night, I argued with Jen in my head about changes. Changes can be for the worse just as easily as for the better, I was going to tell her, and if they're for the worse, you should resist them. But she didn't give me a chance to tell her anything before she started talking. Her voice had the high, hurried sound that means she's afraid I won't like what she's going to say.

"I know you expected me to go shopping with you and Mother Saturday, but my math teacher has a new microchip in his computer that gives him advanced graphic capabilities. He's invited three of us over to show us some stuff, and I'd really like to go, because—well, he's so nice to me, Case. Would you feel awful going alone with Mother?"

"No, that's okay," I said, glad to be generous about one day since I'd made Jen give up a whole summer for me. "Mother and I'll get along fine alone." I crossed my fingers, hoping that was true, and added, "After all, she is my mother."

"See, I hate to keep saying no to him when he's been so nice to me," Jen kept explaining. "You really don't mind?"

"No, you go ahead and have fun," I said grandly.

· · ·

What you see from the train window between Stamford and New York City are lots of trees streaming by or else ugly factories sprawled alongside the tracks and warehouses that look like boxes

79

with dead window panes. Where there aren't broken windows, there's cracked concrete. Close to the city a line-up of apartment buildings begins, which I like better because you can catch a glimpse of a little boy cradling a doll or a window with bright orange geraniums. The car I sat in was mostly empty. In warm weather, New Yorkers head out of, not into, the city. The train burrows underground for the last part of the ride and rumbles through an endless eerie tunnel until it finally stops beside the station platform.

Mother was waiting for me. She looked as boxy and energetic as ever. I gave her an enthusiastic hug and kiss and asked where we were going shopping. When she named the store, I groaned.

"What's wrong with it?" she asked. "They have the best selection of basic kid clothes in town."

"I'm not a basic kid anymore. Haven't I grown out of that place yet?" I asked her.

"Case, have you gotten into high fashion while I wasn't looking?"

"Not really," I said. I wasn't about to wear something that would get me either mocked or envied in school, or anywhere else for that matter; it was just the principle of the thing. We'd started going to that store when we lived in Brooklyn, and it made me feel like a little kid to be going there still. "I'm just tired of the place."

"If you're going to give me a hard time today, you can get right back on that train and go home," Mother said. "I've had a rough week, and my nerves are shot."

"Actually," I said, "I've been looking forward to this shopping trip."

"Good. So have I." She smiled and ran her hand lightly over my freshly washed hair. "You're looking healthy. I suppose you're having a ball living on that derelict boat?"

"The boat's fine, but I hate being half a family."

"You'll get used to it," she said cheerfully.

I took advantage of her cheer to ask if we could eat lunch in a really nice place.

"So long as you're satisfied with a really nice moderate-priced place," she said.

We walked arm-in-arm through city streets that were soft as pigeon feathers with summer. Even the air was downy. Not that it slowed people much. Everybody strode along, and traffic dashed grimly through the crossing before the lights changed. New York is lively, but not very nice. I saw a taxi driver screaming at a poor, stooped-over old lady. Mother and I both laughed when the old lady gave him the finger and continued on her way. A teenage boy wearing earphones walked past bare-chested with his box on his shoulder, lost in the music. It was a long hike, and we saw representatives of half the world's nations along the way.

"So how's Gerry doing?" Mother asked. "Any sales yet?"

"Not yet. He's producing a lot, and his agent keeps telling him it's good and will sell eventually. Do you think it will?"

"It's probable," she said. "He usually succeeds at whatever he tries—eventually."

"How come you never said that to him?"

"What do you mean?" she asked me in surprise. "He knows he's competent."

"I don't think he knows you think he is," I said. "You know what he said about a friend of his?"

"What?"

"That what he likes about this friend of his is that the friend believes in him."

"This friend," Mother said. "Are you talking about Miki?"

"How do you know about Miki?" I was startled because I'd been trying hard not to give Dad away.

"Gerry and I use the telephone, too," Mother said. "Not as much as you and Jen do, but we keep in touch."

"You do? And you don't care about Miki?"

"Should I? Gerry has a right to have friends. If he likes her, she's probably nice."

"Yes, she's nice," I said. "And pretty."

"Oh?" Mother gave me a quick look. "Are you worried, Case?"

"Mother," I said, "did you decide you don't love him anymore?"

"I still love him. What's that got to do with anything?"

"It doesn't?" I was amazed. The things adults will say!

"Case, Gerry and I are separated because he's changed and I haven't. He used to think it was great that I was an ambitious, hard-working career woman. He used to cheer me on. Now he's decided I'm a driven woman. He wants me to applaud that he can't settle down to one career and do something with it. It's just as much his fault we're separated as mine, really."

I frowned. It sounded logical. "But what about moving to New York? He hates New York, and you wanted him to—"

"I don't want to discuss it," Mother snapped. "What goes on between my husband and me is private."

"It shouldn't be," I said, "because if affects me—Jen and me both."

Mother simmered down. "Listen," she said wearily. "Can't we talk about something neutral—like the weather?"

"The weather's nice," I said. "But if you really love Gerry, you could figure out a way to live together. That's all." I held up my hand to halt her explosion. "That's all I'm going to say. The weather's really perfect today, isn't it?"

"You know," Mother said, "I made up my mind to get through today without any major battles with you, but you've got to do your part."

"I will." I even took her arm and kissed her cheek to show how glad I was to be with her.

Saturday night Mother took Jen and me to an outdoor concert. The music was really heavy. I fell asleep during the second half of it. Next day, Mother walked me to the station alone. It was then that she let me have it. She started very cautiously, "Case, I want to talk to you about something. Would you please hear me out before you get defensive?"

"What now? I thought we weren't going to fight."

The shopping turned out to be fun. I liked everything Mother bought for me—summer pants and shorts and tops, plus a fantastically feminine peasant skirt and blouse, which she said I really didn't need, but she couldn't resist because it looked so cute on me. I couldn't wait to show it to Jen, and I really did appreciate that Mother got it for me even though it wasn't practical.

So over lunch I was feeling warm and daughterly, and she was relaxed. I'd picked a Chinese restaurant that turned out to be good, and she dug into her shrimp with lobster sauce and confided that her new boss was a tyrant.

"It's hard to keep my temper, Case," she said. "Yesterday he dumped yet another sticky problem on my desk with a 'You should be able to handle this,' as if it were small enough to fit my limited mental capacity. What he's really doing is sticking me with the problems he can't solve and then taking credit when I get them done right. I had such an urge to belt him one, you can't imagine."

"You could quit and get a job near home," I suggested.

"I'm not a quitter."

"But if things aren't going right at work and you really love us—"I began, but she interrupted me.

"At the moment," she said, "I'm satisfied with the way things are."

"Jen and I aren't satisfied with the way things are."

"You may not be. Jen is. She loves her school."

"Oh, big deal—computers."

"It's more than computers, Case. It's finding people she has something in common with. She's finally part of a group."

"Jen's an individual," I said. "She doesn't need to be part of a group."

83

"That's what you think. You should have seen her face shine last night when she got two phone calls, one from a girl and one from a boy. Sure, all she talks with them is computer gobble-degook, but it's some practice in social behavior, at least."

"I didn't know you were worried about Jen's social behavior," I said uneasily.

"Well, do you think it's normal for a fourteen-year-old girl not to have any friends and to spend all her time with her little sister?" Mother asked.

"Jen and I like being together. She thinks I'm good company."

"No doubt, but—oh, come on," Mother said impatiently. "Next thing you know we'll be at it again. Let's get out of here."

She paid the bill. We divided the bags of clothes between us, then went outside, where we made some more weather conversation.

"We're not, but I am your mother, and you should be willing to listen to my advice."

"Advice about what?"

"That computer camp Jen wants to go to. She really wants it bad, Case. It's a special honor even to be asked, especially at the end of the term, and then to get a scholarship—"

"She didn't get the scholarship yet."

"Sure she did. Didn't she tell you? Her math teacher got her the whole works, scholarship and all. Another kid who can't go was supposed to have it."

"She'd rather spend the summer with me," I said, even though I knew it was a lie before the words were out of my mouth. "Maybe they'd let her go for a week," I added.

Mother's a tough lady. "Don't be silly," she said. "It's a six-week program. She'd be back for part of August."

I didn't know what to say. My throat felt sore all of a sudden. I hoped I was getting sick, really sick so that Jen wouldn't want to go off to computer camp and leave me behind. "She can go next year," I said. "Next year we won't be on the way to getting

84

divorced, and I might not need her around so much as I do now.''

Mother looked away from my misery and said, "If Jen refuses them, she won't get another chance next year. Certainly not with a scholarship thrown in. Aren't you proud that they think enough of your sister to offer her a fantastic opportunity like this?''

"Sure I'm proud,'' I said. "I've always been proud of Jen.'' I was struggling to hold back my tears, and most of the rest of Mother's arguments got lost in the buzzing in my head.

"Well?'' she asked. I didn't answer. I wasn't going to give in to her because she was mean to have bought me all those nice clothes and taken me out to lunch and talked about herself yesterday, and all because she wanted to set me up for this pitch about Jen. She should've come right out and told me what a selfish rotten kid I am. Then I could have defended myself.

Well, I'm not deliberately a monster, and I do love my sister. So when I got back to the boat, I reluctantly found my red sticky paper and cut out a fat red heart. I pasted the heart on a folded piece of paper. Inside I wrote that I was proud Jen got the scholarship for computer camp and I really wanted her to go and have a good time. I constructed an envelope from a bigger sheet of paper and mailed it on my way to school Monday morning.

You'd think I'd get rewarded for acting like such a good kid. I mean if life were fair, things should have improved for me. But they didn't. Tuesday it rained hard. Norma was supposed to come to the boat with me after school, but at lunch she said she didn't want to walk all that way in the rain. "You never want to come to the boat,'' I said. "Don't you like me anymore?''

"I don't like the rain,'' Norma said. "I don't like the boat much, either. Why don't you come to my house?''

"I always go to your house,'' I said. "For a change, I was hoping you'd come to mine.''

"You don't have a house; you have a boat,'' she said.

So we had a fight. We made up before lunch was over, but I had the aftertaste of fight in my mouth, and fighting with Norma makes me feel almost as bad as fighting with Jen.

Wednesday morning it was still raining, and I dropped my math homework on the street and stepped on it, which naturally put the wet muddy print of my sandal right over everything, but you could still read the answers.

"Do it over," my math teacher said to me.

"Why? I'm not going to learn anything from doing it again."

"It's an insult to a teacher to hand in work like this," he said. Hard to believe I could ever have thought he was cute.

"I could have copied from someone in homeroom and you'd never have known," I pointed out. "At least I did my own work. And how come you're giving homework when the term's almost over, anyway?"

"I'll see you after class," he said, and he didn't mean to chat. He made me sit there and do the whole set of examples over from the book before he dismissed me. "I don't like your attitude, Case," he said. Never again will I fall for a teacher because of his looks.

That evening before dinner I was sitting in the saloon on the boat, staring out the sliding glass windows at the rain and wondering if Jen had gotten my letter yet. I'd called her Sunday evening to say I really wanted her to go to computer camp, but I couldn't tell if she believed me or not. She'd just kept saying, "Oh, Case!"

Brian came along in a yellow slicker with a slip of paper in his hand. "Hi Brian," I called, popping out of the open hatch to hail him. "Who are you looking for?"

"Message for Gerry," Brian said.

"I think he went to call his agent. He should be back any minute. Come on in and talk to me a while, please?"

"Can't. The head in this guy's boat isn't working, and he's got five little kids who need that toilet. I promised to help him. Listen, when's your sister coming next?"

"I don't know," I said gloomily. "She may not have time to

come again. She's going to computer camp for six weeks."

"Hey," Brian said. "Don't feel bad. Like I told you, you can have a big brother instead of a sister this summer. You might like it more than you think."

He was so nice that I burst into tears.

"Come on," he said. "There's enough water coming out of the sky already. You trying to flood the place?"

"Everthing's mud, and I hate mud," I said.

He did his best to comfort me quickly. Then, before he took off, he asked for Jen's phone number. "So I can give her a call before she leaves," he said.

"Do you like her a lot? I asked him.

"Sure, I like her," he said. "You jealous?"

"No," I said honestly, but I was impressed. Pretty as Jen is, I didn't expect boys to be interested in her yet, because she's so shy and quiet. Computer camp and boys! I was getting crowded out of her life fast.

Gerry came in later. Rain dripped from the curly fringe of his hair. He never remembers to wear a raincoat. As he was toweling off his head, he told me, "Brian said the real-estate agent wanted to talk to me, so I called. It looks like we've got a buyer, Case."

"The house is going now, too?" I cried.

"Sounds pretty definite this time." He looked sorry as he draped the wet towel around his neck. "They're willing to pay the asking price, and Mrs. Delaney bets they'll have no trouble getting a mortgage."

"Rats," I wailed. "Double rotten lousy rats. Oh, Daddy, can't you do something?"

He shook his head. We communed in silence until Miki's cheery voice called, "Ahoy, there, *Jokester*. Anybody aboard?"

"We don't want to speak to her now, do we, Dad?"

"Sorry, honey. I invited her for supper," he said. "You don't really mind, do you?"

I didn't answer him, just dug out my water-repellent poncho, yanked it on and left. I said "Hi" to Miki as I marched past her on my way to the phones. Of course, I hadn't taken any money; so I had to go back to square one for some change. I jumped the three steps down into the saloon and saw Miki sitting next to my father with one arm around his shoulder and the other hand patting his leg. He was telling her—not about the sale of the house that I thought he felt as bad about it as I did—but about a near miss of a sale of his cartoons to a major newspaper chain.

"You've got to have faith in yourself," Miki was saying. "It'll happen for you. I know it will."

How was I going to immunize him to moral support like that? No way. I got my change, told them I'd be right back and returned to the phones to call my sister. My brain can only deal with so many problems before it goes numb. I was so numb that I didn't even react when nobody answered the phone. I put some of the change from the phone call that didn't go through into the candy machine and comforted myself by eating two chocolate bars, one after the other.

The world was as dark and sad as I was as I dragged back to the boat. The overhead lights were caught in nets of mist, and the black water reflected streaks of light. Even the boats with lamplight glowing in their portholes looked lonely in their slips under the sifting rain. I stopped short when I heard them laughing inside *The Jokester*. No way could I join them aboard. I counted the money I had left and turned around for the second time to try the phones. This time someone answered, but it was Mother.

"How come you're home so early?" I asked.

"Oh, hi, Case. Yes, for a change I got home before Jen."

"You all right?" I asked, detecting a downbeat in her voice.

"More or less. How would you like it if I came and spent a week or two on the boat with you and your father?"

"What? Don't you have to work?"

"I'm taking a vacation."

"Oh," I said, still too surprised to react. "Did you know the house is sold, really sold this time?''

"Yes, the agent called me. . . . Wouldn't you like having your old mother around for company after Jen leaves? Incidentally, I saw your note to Jen. Very sweet. I'm proud of you. I know it's a big sacrifice.''

"Yes," I said. I was thinking of Miki and Mother on the boat together and wondering if that was going to be good or bad. "Did you ask Dad about spending your vacation with us?''

"No. Don't you think he'll be pleased?''

"I don't know. He might have plans.''

"You mean, to take the boat somewhere? But that would be fun.''

"No, the engine still doesn't work right. It's not that. It's— you better talk to him.''

"Don't you want me around, Case?" Mother asked.''

"Of course, I want you around. I mean, you're my mother.''

"And that's all I get points for, huh?''

"No, listen. I love the clothes we bought. Everybody said I looked slick in that red peppermint shorts thing.''

"Tell your father to call me tonight, okay? And don't despair if I wind up spending a week with you. I won't get in your way.'' Mother sounded hurt. She hadn't understood. I'd tried to be tactful and had made her feel bad. So what else was new? I went back to the boat too depressed to care who was there.

I wished I'd been able to talk to Jen. Jen would know what to say to Mother. Jen never hurt people's feelings the way I did. I tried to imagine Mother and Miki and Dad together on *The Jokester*. Would they fight with each other? Adults are so weird. For all I knew, Mother and Miki might get to be good friends. Whatever, I wasn't going to have to wait long to find out.

# ·TEN·

LUCKY FOR ME, JEN'S computer camp was to start on a Monday. That gave us a last weekend together, which we were going to spend in New York. However, Mother was in a hurry to begin her boating vacation and wouldn't let Jen and me stay in the apartment alone. All of a sudden we were having an all-member family reunion aboard *The Jokester*. It was quite a weekend. Incredible is how I'd describe it.

Jen came to the boat Friday directly from her last final, equipped with those tabs you paste behind your ears that work by osmosis. The astronauts use them to keep from having motion sickness. The first thing she said to me when she got off the train was, "Case, you're the best sister. Sending me that heart was so nice. I wasn't going to listen to you after the phone call, because I know you really don't want me to go, but Mother said I had to stop treating you like a baby and acting like you can't manage without me."

"Umm," I said, wishing Mother hadn't butted in. I was prepared to listen to more about my noble sacrifice, but Jen was done with it. She's too unselfish to appreciate how hard it is for me to give up something I want.

"Don't worry about me," I told Jen bravely. "Norma invited me to stay with her the first week you're gone."

"This coming week?" Jen said. "You mean you're leaving Mother and Gerry alone on the boat? Wow!"

90

"What do you mean, wow?" I asked. "What's the difference whether I'm here or not? They'll probably get along better without me."

Jen took her time thinking that one over. We were sitting up on the fly bridge of *The Jokester* in our bathing suits, getting tanned. At least I was getting tanned. Jen has to slather herself with sun screen to avoid burning; so all she gets is pink on her nose and cheeks. I watched two kids fishing from a rowboat in the middle of the channel. Sure enough, they got chased by an obnoxious power boat heading out into the sound. The power boat's big horn blasted our ear drums.

"Norma and I may produce a puppet show and charge admission to the kids in her neighborhood while I'm there," I told Jen. "This summer I plan to make a lot of money. Brian says he'll pay me to help him with boat-washing jobs."

"What do you need a lot of money for?" Jen asked idly.

"So when you come back in August we'll be able to do things together without having to beg from the parents."

Jen smiled. "That's nice, Case . . . I wonder if Mother knows about Miki yet."

"She knew about her all along. Dad told her," I said. "And I asked him if he was going to feel funny having both his wife and his girlfriend around. You should have heard him lecture me about Miki not being his girlfriend. He acted like I was insulting him or something."

"I wonder if Mother is going to like her," Jen said.

"Mother being Mother, she'll probably do something absolutely incredible like advising him to marry Miki."

"She's not that crazy," Jen said.

"We'll see," I said. Mother was due to arrive the next morning.

Brian hailed us, and Jen stood up to talk to him. "How about going swimming with me?" he asked her as he gave her the once-over. "I'm off this afternoon."

"No, thanks, Brian," Jen said. "I want to spend every bit of this weekend with Case."

"Case can come, too," he said, but she shook her head. All he got was a promise she'd write him a letter from camp. In exchange, he said he'd take good care of me while she was gone.

"Don't you like him?" I asked after he'd left.

"Sure I do. But I wish he wouldn't look at me that way."

"He looks at you like you're sexy."

"Well, I'm not ready for it," she said. I was relieved to hear that computers were still my main competition.

"Let's go say good-bye to our old house, Jen," I suggested. The people who'd bought it had gotten their mortgage and were going to close on the house Monday, while Mother was in Stamford. "It's our last chance to see it while it's still ours."

"If you want to," Jen said agreeably.

"Don't you care about saying good-bye?"

"It's just a house, Case, not a person. I don't get as emotionally involved with *things* as you do."

While we were changing into shorts and T-shirts for the walk to the house, I confided, "I'm going to miss you a lot when you're gone. Can you call me from camp every night?"

She hugged me and said, "I'll do the best I can."

"You know what I'd really like," I pushed it. "I'd like to have a ceremony, sort of. I mean, to say good-bye to the house." I waited for her to look disgusted, but she didn't.

She even said, "All right. Why don't you make a heart, and we'll sign our names and paste it on the tree in the backyard or something."

"It would wash off, but that's a good idea," I encouraged her. I mean, she was trying hard to please me. "We could bury something that matters to us. Like, I know what I could bury." I didn't want to say what, but I cued Jen, "Some part of us that would always be there no matter where we are."

"Case," Jen said, "you know we were going to be separated anyway. In three years I'll be going off to college, and—"

"But three years is forever. It's getting separated now that I hate."

"Even if we're not physically close, we'll be close in the way that counts most, won't we?" she said.

"I want you where I can touch you, not close far away," I told her.

She just smiled at me in a loving way and asked me what I was going to bury.

"You'll see," I said. "Let's leave it till tomorrow morning, when it's cool, and just sit around and read today. Okay?"

"Okay," she said. "How about if I bury my old glasses? I don't need them anymore now that I'm used to the contacts."

"Fine," I said. But later when we were raising the cocktail table and flipping it open to turn it into a dining table in the saloon, I had a funny-sad thought. Jen was going to bury a piece of herself that she was glad to leave behind, but what I was going to leave was something I still loved. It figured. Everything seemed to be going hard or wrong or bad for me.

While we were eating our chili and beans for dinner, Gerry said to Jen, "I still don't understand how your mother got a vacation. She told me she was advised not to take one this summer because of the new job. What did she say she plans to do on the boat all week?"

"She mentioned taking care of some house stuff," Jen said. "Before the people move in, you've got to decide what to do with all the furnishings, don't you?"

"Right, we do," he agreed. "You girls better pick out what you want to keep. Maybe you and your mother could have a garage sale, Case. That'd keep her busy. I warned her that the boat's not seaworthy and that nothing much is going on here at the marina."

"She can read and sleep," Jen said. "I think she's exhausted. The job's a lot harder than she thought."

"I'd *never* do a garage sale with our things," I said indignantly.

"I'm not going to sell part of my family to strangers. Besides, I'm going to be at Norma's all week."

"Just a thought," Gerry said.

We'd just finished the dishes when Miki arrived with a can of nuts that one of her nursery-school kids had given her. "I break out when I eat nuts. You guys want them?"

Gerry was sampling a handful when he said casually, "Hey, Miki, did I tell you Marian's coming to spend her vacation week on the boat?"

"You're kidding," Miki said. She looked from Jen to me as if she expected us to tell her he was joking. Then she gave a shaky laugh and said, "Looks like you'll have a full house with your daughters in the bow bunks and your wife—where's she going to sleep?"

Jen suddenly got up and disappeared through the hatch onto the aft deck. "I'm going to take a walk," she said, but I ignored the look she bent back down to give me. I wanted to hear Gerry's answer.

"Hadn't thought about it," he told Miki amiably. "This couch in the saloon opens up. The boat'll sleep six in a pinch, you know."

"Do you want her here?" Miki demanded.

"It depends on how it works out," he said. "The only thing I really want right now is to sell some cartoons."

Miki smoothed her hair back. She looked distracted. Finally she shrugged. "Are we going to try that piano bar I told you about, or would you just as soon forget it?"

"No, hey, let's go," he said. "Tonight we've got a built-in baby-sitter, Case-approved and all."

Jen came back from her solo walk quickly, and Dad and Miki went off together. I sat on the couch beside Jen, watching the small-screen TV with my chin on my knees. "I don't think Dad likes Miki as much as Miki likes Dad," I said.

"Well, it's obvious she doesn't think he's too old for her or

94

too married or anything," Jen said. "It's a good sign that Mother wants to spend time on the boat with him, though."

"Did she say anything to you about it?"

"She said you and she had a serious talk Saturday. She said you gave her something to think about."

"I did?" As I remembered it, she made me do all the thinking.

When I got ready for bed, I took Bearheart into the head and got out the first-aid kit. Bearheart looked a little ratty from all the nights he'd spent in my bed. I'm sort of a restless sleeper. He had a big red felt heart sewn over the bare spot on his belly and a little black felt heart over the glass eye he'd lost. As gently as I could, I bandaged him round and round until he looked like a small mummy and the gauze was used up.

"What's in there?" Jen asked as I came out of the head.

"What I'm going to bury tomorrow," I said. I tucked Bearheart into my bunk, climbed in beside him, and in the dark, for the very last time, I kissed him good-night.

It was so hot and humid the next morning that my top was soaked even before we left the marina. Jen was carrying the shovel Brian had found for us, but she looked cool. The "Sold" sign was plastered right across the board that said, "House for Sale." It gave me a shock. It was really happening to me. I used to think nothing very bad could ever happen to me, but I'd lost faith in my luck. What could be worse than losing your mother, house and sister? It was tragic, and now I was burying Bearheart, and that was like burying a piece of my old self. I didn't really know why I was doing it, except to prove to Jen that I could take change. But I couldn't; so who was I fooling?

The only spot in the backyard soft enough to dig was the little patch where Dad used to plant a couple of tomato plants each June. Nothing there this year, of course. "Want me to dig?" Jen asked me.

"We'll take turns," I said. "I want a good deep hole so that they won't plant a rosebush or something and find Bearheart."

95

"Bearheart? You're burying Bearheart? Are you sure, Case?" Jen sounded as if I was committing a crime.

"If I miss him, I can come into the yard some dark night and dig him up again."

"No, you can't."

"Okay, so I can't. But it doesn't matter. He's my childhood, and when you don't have a family anymore you can't be a child."

Jen frowned. "Oh, Case!"

"Don't give me a hard time," I said. "That's how I honestly feel. Now let's dig and get back to the boat before Mother gets there."

When the hole was very deep, I put Bearheart to rest on top of Jen's old glasses. "Farewell," I said, reciting what I'd prepared in my head while I was bandaging him. "You've been a wonderful bear-pal to me. I hope you live forever in bear heaven, where you deserve to go. Farewell." I thought it was a beautiful speech, and I glanced at Jen to see if she was impressed. She looked embarrassed. Oh, well, what can you expect from a girl who likes computers?

Mother had already arrived when we got back to the boat. "You'll never guess who else is coming," she said as we kissed each other hello.

"Who?" I asked, thinking Mother looked old in baggy jeans and a loose shirt with the gray in her hair showing and sunshine pointing up the lines in the face.

"Your grandmother. Can you believe it? She swore she'd never visit us again after she and I had the big fight. But she called to say she's between jobs and wants to see us. She says she's planning to stay a couple of weeks, even if the city is unendurable in the summer, and even if she's afraid to go out in the streets for fear of being mugged."

"She was always afraid to go out in the streets," Jen said. "She kept Case and me locked in the apartment half the time when we lived with her in Brooklyn."

"But where's she coming?" I asked. "*Here,* to the boat?"

"Your father says it's okay," Mother said.

"Is that what you heard, Marian?" Gerry asked as he climbed down from the fly bridge. "What I said was that I could tolerate her if you could."

"I'm not sure I can," Mother said. "Listen, Gerry, I know this is your turf. If you want, I'll just take Case and Mother to my apartment after Jen goes off to camp on Monday, or maybe Tuesday after the house closing at the lawyer's office."

"Not necessary," he said. "I'll just make myself scarce if she starts getting to me. There's a chance I may do a lot of sailing, anyway."

"With your friend Miki?" Mother asked.

"Right. Incidentally, did your mother give any reason for this sudden change of heart toward us?" Gerry asked.

"She's coming to see the girls, basically. I told her Jen was going off to camp, but she said she'd make do with Case."

I groaned.

"Grandma probably thinks she's going to glue the family back together," Jen said.

"I bet you're right. She probably thinks it's her duty," Mother said. "*That's* why she's going back on her word. Of course. Very shrewd of you, Jen."

"When's she due to arrive?" Dad asked.

"Tomorrow. She expects me to meet her flight. Could you possibly lend me the car, Gerry?"

"I'll lend you the car, but I'm warning you, the first time your mother asks why I'm no longer a responsible wage earner, I'm throwing her off the fly bridge."

"I'll help you," Mother said. "She'll have a hemorrhage when she finds out I quit my job."

"You quit?" Dad asked. "Why?"

"You were right. He was impossible to work for."

"I'm sorry. God, what are you going to do now, Marian?"

97

He sounded really concerned.

"Well," she said. "There are a few possibilities . . ." She stopped talking and looked at me.

"Case, let's go take a shower," Jen said.

"Now?"

"We're all hot and sweaty from our walk," Jen said. "Come on."

"You go first, Jen," I said.

She raised one eyebrow and looked at me hard. I grudgingly left the parents to discuss our futures between them, hoping they'd handle them with care this time.

"Did you know she quit?" I asked Jen when we were alone.

"She feels terrible about it, Case. She feels like a failure. Don't say anything to her about it. She's supersensitive on the subject."

"It must be tough," I said. "Like . . ." I couldn't think of what it would be like. Not even failing a test would be that bad, I guessed.

"Well, is she going to quit New York City, too, then?" I asked Jen.

"No telling what she'll do. We'll just have to see what happens."

While I waited for my turn to use the stall shower in the head off Gerry's stateroom, I imagined how it would be when Grandma arrived tomorrow. It'd be bad, most likely, because Grandma makes everybody angry. Having Grandma on the boat was bound to bring Fourth of July on early, especially when she met Miki. What an awesome event that was going to be! I decided to call up Norma immediately and put off my visit so as not to miss the fireworks.

98

# ·ELEVEN·

I PUT ON MY favorite shorts and a clean shirt, but Jen was taking forever to choose between a skirt and a sunback dress. "How come you're so interested in how you look all of a sudden?" I asked her.

"Because all of a sudden people are noticing how I look."

"I always noticed. . . . You mean people named Brian?"

"Don't tease, Case," she said. "It's embarrassing."

"What?"

"About Brian." She brushed her hair until the static made it stick up and she had to wet it to get it flat again.

"Listen," I said. "Grandma's coming tomorrow, and I don't want to miss that scene. If you want to hang out with Brian after she gets here, it's okay with me."

"Well, he may not be on duty tomorrow, but I did kind of put him off."

"He'd be glad if you put him on again," I said, and she muttered something like she hoped so. It shook me to realize she really did want to be with him.

When we finally climbed onto the aft deck, the big meeting between Mother and Miki had already happened. No signs of battle. In fact, the three of them were talking together like old friends. Gerry was sprawled on a deck chair with his hands clasped behind his curly head and a pumpkin grin on his face. Mother sat in the other deck chair, looking kind of square and frowsy compared to Miki, who was perched up high on a turned-around captain's seat at the control panel. Miki had one slim leg folded so she could use her knee as a chin rest while the other leg swung loose and naked. Her painted toenails didn't quite reach the floor. Norma says my mother's an interesting-looking woman, but in a beauty contest with Miki, Mother didn't have a chance.

"Don't you look pretty," Miki said, spotting Jen in her sun-back. "Got a hot date with Brian?"

Jen looked pained. Mother rescued her.

"You look nice and cool after your showers, girls. Why don't you get cushions or something and sit on the floor?"

"It's crowded up here," Jen said. "I think I'll read in the saloon." She smiled at Miki and retreated.

Not me. I plopped down cross-legged in the middle of the action with my back against the hatch door where I could watch all three of them as they talked.

"Anyway," Miki said, apparently continuing a conversation that Jen and I had interrupted, "I really admire successful business women. That's a whole other thing from my job. I mean, nurturing comes naturally to a woman, but being a financial analyst—that's so masculine."

"Being a nursery-school teacher must be rewarding," Mother said politely.

"Definitely. Of course, I don't let my job run my life. Besides sailing, I've got all these other interests. Like, would you believe cake decorating and wine tasting?"

"I'd believe it, yes," Mother said. "And you must do aerobics. Or is it running?"

"I do yoga," Miki said.

"Of course, yoga," Mother said with a knowing smile.

The conversation sagged. Gerry cleared his throat, but before he said anything, Miki asked, "Do you like sailing, Mrs. Ekert?"

"It's Marian," Mother said. "I did ask you to call me Marian, didn't I?"

"Marian is a fair-weather sailor," Dad put in. "She likes it

100

best when there's no wind and the boat doesn't heel."

"It's too bad our boat is so small, or I'd invite you to join us this week," Miki said. "But with Gerry and my brother and sister-in-law and me, there's really no room. Anyway, we'll be going out in all kinds of weather."

"Are you planning to sail all week, Gerry?" Mother asked. "You didn't warn me you'd be gone all the time."

"Just on day trips," he said. "I didn't think you'd care. You said you were coming aboard *The Jokester* to relax. Did you expect me to—"

"You're right," Mother said quickly. "Of course, I don't expect you to entertain me." She turned to Miki and smiled and said, "Tell me more about your boat."

"Well, without Gerry, we'd never have gotten it in shape. He's so handy. It's wonderful that an artistic type like Ger can be so clever with practical problems."

"Gerry's an artistic type? Oh, you mean his cartoon strips," Mother said. "I suppose I've seen him through so many of his incarnations that I don't label him anymore. I can't wait to see what he'll be doing when he grows up."

She laughed but nobody else did.

"Sometimes you sound just like your mother," Gerry said.

"You have to be patient with him, Mrs.—Marian," Miki said. "He just hasn't found himself yet, but when he does, look out, world."

"You seem to know my husband well."

"We've talked a lot," Miki said earnestly. "You can get really close when you have the time to really talk to each other. What's so great about Ger is he's willing to share his innermost thoughts and feelings with a friend. Most men aren't as sensitive as he is."

"Ger's a nice guy," Mother said. "Nobody ever doubted that."

I wondered when Mother had started calling Dad "Ger."

Maybe she'd caught it from Miki.

"Would you women like me to leave while you talk me over?" Dad joked.

"Why don't you go help Miki with that bilge problem she mentioned," Mother said. "No need for you to stay and entertain me. I'm going to stretch out on the bow in the sun and try to get rid of some of this city pallor."

"Maybe you'd like to come over and see *The Skimmer* later," Miki said. "She's a sweet little boat."

"Later," Mother said, giving Miki an abbreviated smile.

Then they all got up and went in different directions, Gerry and Miki off to her boat and Mother back to the bow compartment where she'd dropped her suitcase on my bunk. I trailed after her, passing Jen, who was curled up in the farthest corner of the saloon's couch, reading and cracking her toes. Mother was throwing off her clothes as if she couldn't stand wearing them anymore. She dug out a new bathing suit. It was nice, but she'd have looked a lot better in it if she'd lost a few pounds.

"Why didn't you tell me that woman's after your father?" Mother asked me with her back still toward me.

"It's not his fault," I said. "He needs someone to talk to."

"That's what I thought he had you here for."

"Somebody adult."

"Why didn't you tell me, though?" Mother insisted.

"Because Jen says it's Dad's private business."

"Oh, God!" Mother said. "Look at these bulges. I should be taking aerobics myself." She was poking at her thighs and frowning.

"Anyway, he says she's just a friend," I said.

"Don't worry, Case," she said. "I'm not upset. Why should I be upset that the minute I turn my back on him he takes up with a cute young chick?" She sounded as if she was trying to convince someone, but I wasn't sure who.

"It's not his fault," I said again. "*She* took up with him."

102

Mother nodded. "If I'd quit my job a little sooner—you should have told me to quit my job sooner," she said to me. Then she walked out and up to the deck through the saloon, where Jen was still reading.

She's gone mad, I thought as I dug out the flotation cushions for her to stretch out on. "Thanks, Case," she said, and hugged me briefly when I handed them to her.

I left her sunbathing on the bow and went below to consult with Jen. She lifted her head from her book and said, "Mother may not *want* to be upset, but she sure is."

"How do you know?"

"I can hear it in the way she says she isn't."

"Too bad," I said.

"She's jealous. I guess she didn't expect Miki to be so young and pretty."

"Do you think they might get back together now?"

"It's unlikely," Jen said. "Grandma's coming tomorrow. With Grandma around, it's going to get messy."

"You told Mother you thought Grandma was coming to glue things together," I said.

"What Grandma *means* to do is likely to be very different from what she actually does. When we lived together, she was always criticizing Gerry, telling Mother that she should have done better or not gotten married again at all. . . . Case, I'm ashamed to admit it, but I'm glad you insisted I go to computer camp. I don't want to be on this boat with everybody jammed in on each other. I only wish I could take you with me."

"But I kind of like being in the middle of things," I said.

All Sunday morning Mother stewed about the weather. We were in for another day of thunderstorms, and she was worried about Grandma flying through them and then not being able to land. Also, Mother hates driving in the rain. Jen had bumped into Brian accidentally on purpose, and he'd invited Jen and me

103

to play computer games at his house and promised to deliver us back to the marina by car. I was looking forward to it, but then Mother asked if one of us wouldn't please go with her to pick up Grandma at the airport.

"I'd go," Gerry said, "but she might get confused if we appear together after you told her we'd separated."

"Girls?" Mother begged.

"I'm going to visit Brian," Jen said breathlessly.

"For a girl who never had any social life at all, you certainly have developed an extensive one fast," Mother complained.

"There you go sounding like your mother again," Gerry said. "You've been giving the kid a hard time for years about being a loner, and now that she's become social, you're giving her a hard time about that."

"You're right. I don't know what's gotten into me," Mother said. "Go have a good time, Jen. He *is* a nice boy, isn't he, this Brian?" She looked at Gerry for an answer.

"Very nice, a little mature for Jen, but a decent kid—I hope," he reported.

"Don't worry, Mother," Jen said. "I wouldn't be seeing him if he wasn't nice."

Mother nodded. "Okay. Casc, why can't you go to the airport with me?"

"Do I have to?"

"No," she said, "but I'd appreciate it if you would."

I shrugged. It wasn't often that my mother gave me an option when she asked me to do something. "Okay," I said.

"How come you're giving in so easily?" Mother questioned.

"Because you asked me as if I was a real person," I said.

"Good God!" Mother said. "Don't I always treat you like a real person?"

"No. You treat me like a kid."

"Really? Well, that may be because of the way you act. I'm not at my best with emotional people, especially young ones."

I didn't count that exchange a win for either Mother or me—more like a draw. Anyway, I put on my new peasant skirt and blouse to go to the airport. After all, if you haven't seen your grandmother in a couple of years, you want to make a good first impression on her. I even tied my hair back with a ribbon. Grandma has a thing about messy hair, especially long messy hair. She likes things short and neat.

"So how do you feel about Miki?" Mother asked me when we were off and away in the rain in Dad's car.

"She's okay."

"A bit of a lightweight. At least that was my impression. But, of course, lightweights might be easier to live with."

"I'd rather live with you," I said.

"You would, Case? I thought you didn't like me much."

"Just because you make me mad a lot doesn't mean I don't like you," I said. "Actually, as mothers go, you're okay."

"Really, darling?" I couldn't believe there were tears in Mother's eyes as she glanced at me. "I'm flabbergasted," she said. "I'm bowled over and blown away. I'm so glad I made you come with me, if only to hear that."

I sat there reviewing what I'd said to find out why she'd reacted so strongly. Finally I decided my mother must really love me.

With the thunder crashing and lightning flashing and rain splashing onto the street in huge drops, Mother had to concentrate on her driving. I imagined my grandmother's plane circling overhead. No doubt that would make Grandma angry. Anything that didn't go the way she wanted it to made her angry.

We parked in the short-term parking lot and were soaked by the time we got into the terminal, even though we shared the emergency umbrella from the trunk. Five minutes later the rain stopped. The sun came out. The plane landed on time. Grandma walked through the gate from the plane with the other passengers, and neither Mother nor I recognized her. Grandma was slim. Grandma was slick with her white hair stylishly cut and a blue

105

cotton jump suit showing off her figure.

"Mother, you look smashing," my mother said when this elegant older lady approached us expectantly.

Grandma received Mother's kiss on the cheek as if she wasn't sure she wanted it and gave Mother one in return. Then she said to Mother, "You're looking frazzled, but I'm not surprised, considering what's going on in your life." It was my turn next. She looked me up and down without much enthusiasm and said, "And this is my youngest granddaughter. Where's your sister, Case?"

"She has a date. You'll see her at dinner. We're all going out," I answered. "Gerry and Mother are taking us to the best seafood restaurant in Stamford."

"How nice. Well, do I get a kiss hello or are you just going to stand there gaping at me?" Grandma said.

"I'm not gaping," I said, and kissed her.

"I see you still argue about everything," Grandma said.

"You haven't changed much, either," I said without thinking.

"Case!" Mother said.

"I'm sorry," I offered, even though I wasn't really.

While we were waiting for Grandma's baggage to spill onto the conveyor belt, Mother started babbling about the awful thunderstorm we'd driven through on our way to the airport and how worried she'd been about Grandma's flight.

"That explains why you both look so bedraggled," Grandma said. She had always cared a lot about how things looked. Also proper behavior, manners, obligations, and how much strength of character people had. You know those corsets with steel sticks in them that ladies used to wear in the 1800s? Well, if Grandma were an object, that's the one she'd be.

"How is your new job going, Marian?" Grandma asked in the car.

"Well," Mother began, but Grandma sprang her next question without waiting to hear the rest of Mother's answer.

"You like living in that filthy city?"

"It's no dirtier than any other big city," Mother said. "Probably no worse than Cincinnati." Cincinnati was where Grandma had gone to live when Mother got married. Grandma had been born there.

"I beg to differ with you," Grandma said. "Cincinnati is livable. New York is not. The only good thing I can say about your moving there is that you're not subjecting *both* your daughters to it."

"Jen loves it."

"Does she? And you, Case, do you like that concrete jungle?"

"I want my family together. I don't care where," I said.

Grandma gave me a kindly look. "Poor child. You're at an age when you need a mother around," she said.

The sound of Mother's screech was familiar. She'd yelled "Mother!" just like that all the time when we lived with Grandma in Brooklyn.

"Bringing children into the world," Grandma was instructing Mother firmly, "obligates you to raise them properly."

"We've been raised properly," I said on Mother's side because, with her mind on the driving, she needed help.

Bright sunlight shone on all the puddles in the parking lot at the marina, and white hulls and sails were gleaming. Mother really did look frazzled as she got out of the car. Grandma just walked off down the ramp, leaving us to deal with her two huge suitcases.

"How are we going to fit all this junk on the boat?" I whispered to Mother as I helped her unload the car's trunk.

"She looks so great. I thought maybe she'd changed," Mother said.

"Maybe we could drop one overboard," I said, still talking about the suitcases.

"If only she'd get seasick and go home tomorrow," Mother said.

"Couldn't you just tell her now's not a good time for her to visit?" I asked. "She's sure to make everything worse."

107

"Don't talk about your grandmother that way," Mother said, making a typical adult about-face. Grimly she picked up both suitcases and started down the ramp, which was steep because of low tide. I picked up the tote bag, which was the only thing left. Grandma must have loaded it with rocks.

It turned out not to be rocks but presents. Grandma had bought books for all of us—one on teen-age grooming for Jen, one on career choices (of all things) for me, a do-it-yourself exercise book for Mother (although how she knew Mother was carrying a few extra pounds, I don't know), and for Gerry (would you believe it?) a book on male midlife crisis. "People can always improve themselves," Grandma said when we thanked her.

Dad invited everybody to sit down and relax and have a cocktail. Grandma said she'd like white wine. Dad said he didn't have any wine. All he had was beer and gin. Grandma pursed her lips and made do with orange juice. Jen and I had soda while Mother and Gerry drank beer. He asked Grandma how her plane trip had been.

"Fair," Grandma said, but before he could ask another neutral question, she pounced. "Tell me, if your friend finds a buyer for this boat, where will you go?"

"I expect I'll find *someplace* to live," he said.

Grandma shook her head disapprovingly. "A gypsy life is not good for children. Leads to lack of discipline, and Case certainly is in need of discipline."

"Why?" Gerry asked. "Case is a good kid."

"I wouldn't be so sure. You don't know the temptations unsupervised children face nowadays. A girl without her mother is likely to get into trouble," Grandma said. "You don't *approve* of what Marian's done, do you?"

"You mean quitting her job? I think it's the smartest thing she'd done yet," Gerry said. He opened another beer for himself. Grandma was making him very nervous.

"Marian!" Grandma gasped when she'd recovered from Gerry's accidental bomb. "You gave up your promotion?"

"My boss was impossible," Mother said.

"She won't have any trouble finding a good job," Dad said. "She's a top-notch finance person. Plenty of companies would be glad to get her."

"Thanks," Mother said to Dad. Then she told Grandma, "I already have a position I'm considering, Mother. There's really nothing to worry about."

"Isn't there?" Grandma said. "First I hear you're breaking up your marriage, and then I find out you've thrown over the best opportunity in your life. I think there's plenty to worry about."

"Mother, Gerry and I are not children. We appreciate your concern, but we're really quite capable of managing our own lives."

"Well, I must say you don't appear to be. As the senior member of this family, it is my duty to advise you when you're going wrong. I don't expect you to like me for it. I'm not out to win a popularity contest, just to help."

Miki appeared at that point. She was wearing a jump suit that looked a lot like the one Grandma had on, expect Miki's was open halfway down her chest. Grandma stared at her while Gerry made the introductions.

"Miki's a nursery-school teacher," Dad said helpfully.

"A nursery-school teacher?" Grandma said. "And you go around dressed like that?"

Miki turned pale, and about a minute later, without ever sitting down, she said she'd see us tomorrow and left. Gerry looked sorry to see her go. "If we want to have dinner at that seafood restaurant, we'd better leave soon," he said. We all got up to get ready. Mostly that meant waiting in line to use the head.

# ·TWELVE·

You know the way some things are so awful they're funny? Like Grandma at the restaurant that night. We went very early, at five-thirty, because they don't take reservations, and you have to wait in line after six when the crowd comes. Grandma looked at all the empty tables and said, "Are you sure this is a good restaurant? It doesn't look very popular."

We lucked out on our waitress. She was full of smiles and suggestions about what we should order, as if she really wanted us to enjoy our meal. She even brought an extra basket of hot muffins. I ate four. Usually the parents discourage us from ordering appetizers and dessert, but this being a special occasion, we could have everything. Appetizers, desserts and hot muffins are my favorite foods.

While we were waiting for our first course, Grandma treated us to the gory details of her last case. "Before I went off duty, I reminded the family to keep an eye on the old lady," Grandma said. "She may not have had all her marbles, but she was a sly one. Well, they let her wander out and she got herself into the storm sewer. When they finally found her—"

"Mother, the girls!" my mother interrupted.

"They see worse any night on television," Grandma said, and opened her mouth to continue.

110

"Then you don't have a job anymore?" Gerry interrupted. He sounded alarmed.

"Certainly I have a job. People are always after my services. I start with the mother of a prominent doctor as soon as I return to Cincinnati. The family wanted me immediately, but I told them they'd have to wait." She went back to her description of her ex-patient's death from pneumonia and finished just as our orders arrived.

Grandma and I had the clams casino. Mine were absolutely delicious, but Grandma sniffed at hers and asked the waitress if they were fresh. "Not to worry," the waitress assured her cheerily. "All the fish and seafood comes in fresh daily. Really, I guarantee it." Grandma ate one clam and sent the rest back untouched.

Her entrée was filet of sole. "Overcooked!" she pronounced, and when she sent it back to the kitchen, our waitress stopped smiling and began treating our table like enemy territory. It was embarrassing, for everybody except Grandma.

Dad tried to rescue the party. He waited until Grandma finished telling us that you couldn't trust restaurant food no matter how fancy the place was, and then he asked, "Is this new patient of yours also senile?"

"Oh, yes," Grandma said. "Her daughters are worried because she smokes. Of course, I'll stop that."

"Poor lady," I murmured and Jen kicked me under the table.

Somehow the adults started talking politics. You'd think they'd know better. As soon as Mother, who's our family radical, began to frown, Jen stood up and asked if I wanted to go to the ladies' room with her. I went, hoping our elders wouldn't get kicked out of the restaurant for creating a disturbance before we got to eat our desserts.

"If those ladies weren't senile, they wouldn't put up with having Grandma take care of them," I said to Jen as we walked past the long line of people now waiting for tables.

"But it's got to be a depressing job," Jen said. "Grandma probably needs this vacation."

"Jen," I told my kindhearted sister, "Mother's the one to feel sorry for. She's got to survive a whole two weeks with Grandma."

"You're right," Jen admitted, but her lip was quirking at the corner.

"What's funny?" I asked her.

"I thought you'd give Grandma credit for getting rid of Miki so fast."

"Give her enough time, and Grandma could get rid of anybody. She's a human demolition derby. The parents will never get back together with her around."

"You're still hoping?" Jen asked me with such a look of pity that I walked into the stall and closed the door against her.

Of course I was still hoping. "You see," I explained to Jen when I came out and was washing my hands, watching her in the mirror as she combed her hair, "Mother loves a challenge. I figure competing with Miki might be more interesting than work to Mother."

"But it's not up to Mother alone," Jen said. "Gerry seems to be having a pretty good time on the boat, and if she finds another job in the city—"

"You don't think he really loves her?"

"I don't know," Jen said. "I think he's had enough of the way she puts him down."

"She could change that easier than making herself young and pretty," I said. "And if they make up fast enough, maybe we could get our old house back before those people who're buying it move in."

"Case, please don't expect that everything can go back to the way it was. You're going to be so disappointed," Jen said.

"I'm going to expect the best," I said, "and maybe I'll get it."

Jen sighed and stopped arguing with me.

The political discussion must have been very hot because the

112

adults had stopped talking to each other. Nobody said a word through dessert and not much on our way out of the restaurant.

. . .

Back in the marina, the water was so stirred up that the boats were rocking in their slips. I could tell Jen dreaded going aboard. Grandma didn't look too thrilled, either. "Does it always bobble about like this at night?" she asked.

"Sometimes it gets worse," Gerry said without much sympathy.

Even though it was early in the evening, Mother and Grandma retired to the stateroom that they were sharing for the night. Gerry made up the couch in the saloon for himself and said he was going out for a walk. Jen and I played a few games of backgammon, then decided to go to bed. I expected we'd stay up all night talking, but the boat rocked and rolled, making me feel sleepy and Jen feel ill despite her motion-sickness medicine. I wasted the whole night by falling asleep immediately.

I was drinking juice in the galley the next morning when I saw Dad knock on the stateroom door and ask Mother to hand him out his windbreaker.

Mother yawned, looking fuzzy the way she always does when she wakes up. "Are you going sailing this early?" she asked him when he mumbled something to her.

"Yeah, well, Miki and her brother are planning to see how far we can get in a day."

"You're kidding!" she said. "What are we supposed to do here the whole day without you?"

"You could take everybody to the beach," he said. "You can use the car."

Mother stepped up out of the stateroom, closing the door behind her so Grandma couldn't hear, and whispered, "She hates the beach."

"Well, go on a picnic or find a mall that's open," he suggested. "Come on, Marian. She's *your* mother."

113

"That's not my fault," Mother said gloomily.

We ended up driving to an art gallery. Mother found a notice in the local paper about a reception for some artist she'd heard was good. "He does innovative work," Mother said. I could tell by her tone that she didn't think we were going to like it. "Mostly experiments with pure color," she added, trying to prepare us.

The art gallery was a couple of towns away, and Mother decided to try a shortcut on some back road to avoid the heavy traffic on the highway. "Haven't you learned how to get around Connecticut yet?" Grandma asked when Mother finally gave up and got out the map.

Grandma didn't like the art show much, either, when we got to it. "Scandalous," she said. "Getting people out to see such trash. Any kindergarten child could do better."

"He's trying to say something about color and human emotion," Mother explained, reading from the brochure she'd picked up on the way in.

"A lot of phony business," Grandma said so loudly that people turned around to look at us. Jen cringed, but while I did think Grandma could have been quieter about it, I sort of agreed with her. Those pictures were just scratchy blobs of paint.

"I'm hungry," I said. "Can't we eat lunch soon?"

"You ought to think less about food and more about your figure, Case," Grandma said, making me wish I hadn't put off going to Norma's for a week.

We stopped at a lunchroom, anyway. Mother looked depressed. After we'd ordered our sandwiches, Grandma said, "I really don't think you should have let Gerry go off with that young woman for the whole day, Marian."

"Gerry and I are separated, Mother. He has a right to go off with anybody he likes."

"And are you seeing other men?"

"No need to. Work fills my life," Mother said. "Isn't that what you always wanted for me?"

114

"When you were young. Now that you're responsible for a family, it should come first with you."

"You've certainly changed your tune," Mother said. "Overnight, as a matter of fact. Just yesterday you were upset that I'd given up my wonderful new promotion."

"You could have kept the promotion and your husband if you'd been willing to compromise," Grandma said. "That's the difference between you and me. I know how to compromise." Her voice turned sad, and she continued, "I've seen a lot of families in the past few years—how they are together. And I live alone now. I know what that's like, too."

I didn't know exactly what she meant, but her sigh was plain, and Jen was looking sympathetic. I wondered if Mother still thought it was just her new job that had caused trouble.

We ate dinner on the boat without Gerry. Then Grandma and I watched a sitcom on TV while Jen read a book and Mother sat on the aft deck in the dark. She said she wanted to watch the stars come out. When I went up there to say good-night to her, I found her talking very quietly with Gerry.

"Did you have a good sail, Dad?" I asked.

"Great. I wish this boat was in as good a shape as Miki's."

"Why? Then it would sell, and we'd have to move off."

"You're right," he said. "Soon as Miki's relatives give way, we'll get you on that sailboat, Case. You'll love it." He turned toward Mother and added, "You might enjoy it, too, Marian. It's a pretty stable craft."

"I wonder if Miki'd appreciate your inviting your whole family aboard her boat," Mother said.

"Oh, she won't mind. She likes Case."

"Does she?" Mother looked at me and said, "It's true my youngest offspring is showing signs of turning out well. Even her mouth isn't as big as it used to be."

Coming from my mother, that was pretty close to a compliment, but not close enough to keep me from saying, "If I've got a big

115

mouth, I know who I inherited it from."

"There's the old Case, rotten as ever," Mother said fondly. "Give us a kiss good-night and go to bed now. Hurry before Grandma gets a notion to come out and join the party."

The next morning was doomsday for me. I managed to say farewell to my sister without bursting into tears, which was an achievement considering how much I wanted to bawl and hang onto her. "Have a wonderful time and learn lots," I said as I hugged her. My head knew six weeks doesn't last forever, but the rest of me didn't believe it. "Remember to write me," I told her.

"Twice a week at a minimum," Jen promised, "and every day if I can. Thanks, Case."

"For what?"

"You know," she said. "For letting me go."

I was feeling too satisfied with myself to feel bad while Mother drove us back to the boat. We'd left Grandma there cross-stitching one of the samplers she loves to give people that say things like, "Bless this house." Mother hated them. She said they were tacky.

"How'd you like to do your mother the greatest favor of your life?" she asked me while we were waiting for a light.

"You mean, more than putting off going to stay with Norma for a week?" I asked.

"In addition to that. While I'm on vacation and your grandmother is visiting, I'd like you to. . . ." Mother ran out of breath. She shook her head. "It isn't fair," she said. "I can't even *ask* you to do it. Forget it, Case."

"Ask," I said, curious to hear what she wanted. "I can always say no."

Mother sighed, and then in this terribly timid voice, she asked, "Would you go live in my apartment in New York with Grandma for the rest of my vacation week?"

"Me and Grandma? Grandma and I? Alone? What a bummer!"

"I know. I'm a monster. It's too much of a sacrifice. Forget

116

it," Mother said, but she added, "If only that computer camp weren't such a big deal for Jen, I'd have asked her."

"Jen couldn't do it," I said. "Grandma would chew Jen up into little pieces. I'm the only one tough enough to survive Grandma. . . . Aren't I?"

"I don't know, darling. Are you?"

She'd called me darling. Was that a slip or did she mean it? I thought a second and then I asked, "And then you'd be alone on the boat with Dad?"

"And Miki. She doesn't work during the summer, you know. So I expect she'll be around a lot," Mother said.

"Can I tell you something?" I asked cautiously. "You're going to say it's none of my business, but—Grandma thinks your promotion was what split us up, but, Mother, you told me yourself that it's more than that."

"I know," she said. "I have to convince Gerry that I have faith in him, that I respect his capabilities."

"Right," I said, relieved that she understood.

"Relax, Case. I'll do my best. Don't get your hopes too high, though. It could be too late."

"No, it isn't," I assured her. "You're a lot more person than Miki is. Besides, he's pretty easy to please. You work at it, and I'll do my job keeping Grandma away." It was promising a lot, but I'd been willing to almost kill myself to save the family. Spending a week with Grandma couldn't be *much* worse.

Mother parked the car, and we sat a few minutes working out a strategy so that Grandma wouldn't feel she was being muscled out of the way.

. . .

The next morning Grandma and I set off for New York City carrying the key to Mother's apartment and a hundred dollars, which Mother insisted we use for taxi fares. The white lie we'd told Grandma was that Mother had only planned to spend the weekend on the boat and the rest of her vacation taking me

117

sightseeing, and that Grandma would be doing her duty by re-placing Mother so that she could stay in Stamford and relax. Doing her duty is, as I may have mentioned, one of Grandma's highs. She only gave us a hard time about two items. First, she wouldn't take the taxi money.

"Much too extravagant," Grandma said.

"But, Mother, you won't go on the subway, and the buses make you nervous. How are you going to show Case the city if you won't leave the apartment?" my mother argued. "Believe me, I would have spent the hundred fast if I'd been the one doing the city with Case."

"Whatever you don't use, you can give back," I suggested, and that took care of that one.

The second hangup was clothes. Grandma didn't see how she could manage without her complete wardrobe, and no way could she and I lug those suitcases into the city and up to the apartment and back to the boat again. It took Mother hours to help Grandma select the bare minimum of what she'd need. Finally, Grandma and I set off on the train with one small case apiece.

"It'll be good for your mother to be alone with Gerry for a change—like a second honeymoon. If only that girlfriend of his leaves him alone," Grandma said to me on the train.

I nodded, concentrating on my own problem—how to get along with Grandma for a week. "Listen," I said. "Wouldn't it be fun if each of us picked what we wanted to do, and one day we do what I want and one day what you want?"

"Well, the Museum of Natural History is a must," Grandma said.

"How about the South Street Seaport?" I asked. I explained that you could board the old sailing ships, and that the cobbled streets were full of Fulton Fish Market history and boutiques. When I said you could get a guided tour, Grandma agreed that might be worthwhile.

. . .

118

Now, I'm not saying the next few days were the most fun I've had in my life. Grandma was still in the business of making me over, and that meant a daily struggle for me. She'd say, "How often do you wash your hair, Case?" And when I'd tell her, "Often enough," she'd say she didn't think so, and I should learn to respect my elders and not talk back to them. It was hard to keep my temper with her.

One way I found to get her off my back was to ask her about her own childhood. She liked that—talking about it, not the childhood itself. The way she tells it, she spent most of her time with her hands folded, quietly listening to her elders' conversation. No wonder she's such a pain to live with now.

"Don't you think young people should learn to be independent?" I asked when she was giving me a hard time because I wanted to go my own way in the Metropolitan Museum of Art and meet her by the staircase later.

"Not children," Grandma said.

"How are you going to be independent if you don't start learning when you're a child?" I asked.

"Adults are supposed to teach the younger generation what they need to know. Children can't teach themselves."

I never saw anyone as sure of what she knew as Grandma.

As long as she could use a taxi to get around town and didn't have to be anxious about getting mugged or lost in dangerous neighborhoods where she and I might wind up as morgue statistics, Grandma turned out to be an eager sightseer. I couldn't believe her energy. She had more than I did. But even when she wore me out, I enjoyed exploring the Big Apple. I'd lived in it and close to it, but never really seen much of it. Grandma and I went to one Broadway show—a comedy—and two movies. We took the ferry to the Statue of Liberty and explored Delancey Street and Chinatown and the Brooklyn Bridge—things Grandma said she had always wanted to see but never dared to go to before. By the end of the week, I could have talked her into traveling anywhere.

We spent our last day together at the Bronx Zoo. "You know, Case," Grandma said, right in front of the monkey island, "you've been a very good girl this week."

"Thanks, Grandma. You've been a good girl, too," I answered.

"Well, I must admit I enjoyed myself a lot more than I expected," she said. "You're good company despite your fresh mouth."

"And you're fun even though you're always criticizing everything," I said.

"Criticizing? What do you mean? *I'm* not critical."

"You pick on people all the time, Grandma. You're always telling Jen or Mother or me or even Gerry how we should behave."

"Never!" Grandma said indignantly. "I may think things, but I certainly never say them out loud."

"Really, you do," I said, "but I like you a lot now, anyway."

"It's hard," Grandma said, "to know what's right and not to tell people." She considered. Then she murmured, "Just as well I live alone."

That made me feel sorry for her; so I blurted out, "Sometime you ought to invite Jen and me to visit you in Cincinnati."

"Would you come? Cincinnati's a nice city, you know. You can get around in it without having to use taxis all the time. There are the botanical gardens and the zoo and museums. Other people's grandchildren visit them. I've always felt bad that mine never came. Of course, the plane fare is exorbitant, but. . . ."

"Don't worry," I said. "We'll work something out." I even kissed her, and she liked it. She kissed me back, looking pleased.

Lucky thing even the local train to Stamford only takes an hour. I was so impatient to get home that sixty minutes seemed forever. I missed my parents, and I wanted to find out where things stood between them. Besides, Mother had two letters from Jen waiting

120

for me. I hadn't let her open them and read them to me over the phone in case Jen had written something to me that Mother shouldn't know.

"Stamford always has great fireworks on Fourth of July. We'll be able to see them from the boat," I told Grandma as we were pulling into the station.

Next week Grandma would return to the city with Mother while I'd finally get to go to Norma's. But we were going to celebrate Fourth of July weekend together on the boat, everybody but my sister. If only Jen could come, it would be lovely, I was thinking just before I saw her through the train window. She was standing on the platform next to Mother, waiting for me. I screamed with joy and dashed off the train.

"Did you get sick and have to come home?" I asked her as I hugged her.

Jen laughed. "I'm fine. Lots of people went home for the Fourth, and one of the teachers offered me a ride here. Now you don't have to read my letters. You won't like them, anyway. They're all computer talk."

"Did you and Grandma *really* have a good time together?" Mother asked me in a whisper as we walked down the stairs together. "I couldn't believe those phone conversations."

"Grandma's not so bad if you keep her busy," I said.

"You know, Case, I must say I've underestimated you," Mother said. "You're a terrific kid."

I felt as if I'd just made the honor roll.

"So how did it go?" I asked Mother.

"Well, I took a job in New Jersey," she said. "It's a company that's been after me for a while. Not quite as high-powered as the corporate headquarters' position, but with definite possibilities for me."

"That's not what I want to know," I blurted out.

"I know," Mother said. "You'll hear the rest later." I protested, but she crimped her lips together and wouldn't talk.

121

That evening Jen and I left Gerry and Mother and Grandma sitting on the aft deck while we went up to the fly bridge to wait for the first rockets to go off. Jen said she had something to tell me, and I couldn't wait to hear. I thought it was about Mother and Gerry, but as soon as we were sitting next to each other, Jen said, "Brian kissed me when he saw me this morning."

"He did?" We were leaning on the railing looking at the lights around the harbor, which were on even though the sky wasn't dark enough for the fireworks yet.

"A real kiss," she explained. "I mean, not a hello, a—a kiss."

"So?"

"So I liked it."

"Wow," I said. She started talking about computer camp then and how fascinating it was. I felt funny. We were sitting so close our legs were touching, but I felt far away from her.

"What's wrong, Case?" she asked. "Why are you so quiet?"

"How come Miki didn't show up?" I asked, because I didn't want to answer her question and admit I was still a baby who didn't want her to change.

"I don't know, but Mother doesn't seem to be worried about her anymore. Did you notice how pretty Mother's looking?"

"She is?" I said. I *hadn't* noticed.

I heard the first crack of a rocket going off then, but it fizzled on the ground, and the only brightness in the sky when I looked up was a planet near the horizon and a few early stars. I felt so strange, so mixed up. Even if my parents did get together again, we wouldn't be the same family we were exactly. Brian had kissed Jen, and she liked it. Now it wasn't only going to be computers that took up her time, but boys. I felt as if her train were still pulling out of the station and leaving me behind.

"Let's go down and watch with the family," I said, suddenly wanting to be with them. "We can see almost as well from down there."

"Sure," Jen agreed, and we climbed down the ladder.

Gerry offered me a perch on his lap, but I went to lean over the rail next to Mother's chair. "Shall we tell them now?" Mother asked Gerry.

"Go ahead," he said. "The sooner the better for good news."

"We've decided to team up and try it again," Mother said, "Gerry and I."

"I'm so glad!" Jen said.

"Thank heavens you've come to your senses," Grandma said.

"Case?" Mother questioned. "Aren't you going to say anything? You were the one who fought hardest to keep the family together. Aren't you happy?"

"Sure," I said, "and now can we get our house back?"

"I don't believe this kid!" Mother said just as the first good rocket showered down red-tailed stars on us. We all turned to look and to cheer as the next rocket went off in a cascade of gold.

"You know we sold the house," Mother said then. "We'll look for a new one in New Jersey, somewhere where I have a short commute and Gerry feels comfortable. You'll have to change schools, but that's not so bad as long as we're together."

"*New Jersey?*" I said. "We can't stay in Stamford?"

"No, we can't," Mother said as if I should have known that.

"And I'm going to have to leave Norma behind?" My eyes filled up with tears. I couldn't help it.

"Case, you're impossible," my mother said, and Grandma looked disgusted.

"Honey, there's no way you can get everything you want in this life," Gerry said gently.

"I know that," I said. "But that doesn't stop me from wanting everything."

"That's unreasonable," Mother said. "You ought to be so glad we're together again that the other things don't matter."

"Change is what life's about," Grandma said. "Be glad if the changes aren't all for the worse."

I sniffled my way quietly through the next set of rockets. Boat horns beeped and squealed and blasted the air in applause as red and then green stars burst into spaghetti wiggles. Don't be a baby, I told myself. We only get fireworks once a year. No sense missing them. I could cry about Norma later and feel bad about the house some other time. As to Jen, I'd get used to her being different. Maybe I'd even be different myself some day. After all, I wouldn't stay eleven forever, and there must be *something* good about living in New Jersey.

I concentrated on the bursts of red and blue and gold and white cascading over the harbor from high above us. Glorious white chysanthemums made a bouquet brighter than the real stars, and golden arrows shot from the center of a fiery ball. I could hear the "ahs" from people in other boats when a rocket that looked like fireflies inside a green bottle went off. "Look at that!" we yelled. "Bravo. . . . Beautiful!" At the end, the whole sky filled with swirling lights and the pops of a dozen rockets filled our ears.

When there was nothing left to see, I gave each one of them a kiss and talked them into making a circle so we could end the evening with a group hug.

"Case, you nut," Mother said laughing.

"I thought you told me I was a terrific kid," I said.

"You are," she assured me.

Somewhere on the shoreline, someone's private rocket went off with a breathless whoosh, and when it popped, just above the trees, the flowering of red sparklers was different from all the spectacular fireworks we'd seen, but nice in its own way.

I did want to be positive and make the best of things; so before going to bed, I said, "It was the best Fourth of July celebration ever, and we really had something to celebrate tonight, didn't we?"

"We certainly did," Grandma said.

They all gave me approving looks like they thought I'd grown up suddenly, all except Jen. She knew me better. Later, when she and I were lying in our bow bunks talking, she said, "Well,

124

if the high school I end up in doesn't have a good computer program, I can wait for college. The important thing is we'll be a family again. Right, Case?"

"I guess so."

"You still feel bad about leaving Stamford, don't you?"

"And my best friend, and my grandmother house." I didn't add, "And Bearheart," although I was missing him, too.

"Case, you were really excellent tonight. I was very proud of you."

"I'm not so selfish anymore, am I, Jen?"

"No," she said. "You're just not good at letting things you love go; that's all."

"At least I get to keep you for a few years more," I said.

"Good-night, little sister," she whispered. Her voice had a catch in it that made me smile as I fell asleep.